HIS HANDS SHOT OUT
TO FASTEN ON HER ARMS . . .

Shaking her slightly, his eyes burning with frustration and temper, Scott proceeded to bawl her out for slipping away from his protection.

Jennifer stared up at him, dazed. She must be crazy, she thought dizzily. She didn't even hear what he was saying; all she was conscious of was the touch of his hands on her bare arms, of his nearness. *She wanted him to kiss her!*

She wanted him to kiss her! As she silently admitted it, Jennifer couldn't evade the hard painful twist of her heart inside her ribs. Of all the awful things to have happened! She had let herself fall in love with Scott Mitchell . . . !

More Romance from SIGNET

CAPTURE
MY LOVE

by
Mary Ann Taylor

A SIGNET BOOK
NEW AMERICAN LIBRARY
TIMES MIRROR

SIGNET TRADEMARK REG. U.S. PAT. OFF. AND FOREIGN COUNTRIES
REGISTERED TRADEMARK—MARCA REGISTRADA
HECHO EN CHICAGO, U.S.A.

SIGNET, SIGNET CLASSICS, MENTOR, PLUME AND MERIDIAN BOOKS
are published by The New American Library, Inc.,
1301 Avenue of the Americas, New York, New York 10019

FIRST SIGNET PRINTING, NOVEMBER, 1977

1 2 3 4 5 6 7 8 9

PRINTED IN THE UNITED STATES OF AMERICA

To Marrijane, as always,
this book is lovingly
dedicated

1

————◆————

"Do I understand you correctly, Mr. Hudson, are you seriously suggesting that I accompany a young woman, a complete stranger, on a trip to Europe for four weeks?" Scott Mitchell eyed his boss uneasily.

Henry Leland Hudson glowered at the young man and clamped down on the cigar in his mouth. Leaning back in his chair, he said brusquely, "Mitchell, let's get this straight right from the outset, it'll save any misunderstanding. I'm not suggesting, I'm *ordering* you to go! And she isn't a complete stranger, not to me, anyhow. She's my niece. Don't get the idea that I'm offering you a vacation jaunt. I want you to go along to act as a . . . well, a bodyguard, a protector."

Scott's eyebrows rose sharply. "May I ask why she needs a bodyguard, or, as you put it, a protector?"

Hudson pursed his small mouth around his cigar, and his three chins wobbled. For a moment he didn't speak, looking levelly at Scott from the opposite side of the shining office desk. Then, removing the cigar to set it in the ashtray, he said, "She's the daughter of John Lemoyne Cartwright. Does that answer your question?"

So that was it! The daughter of the eccentric millionaire scientist. Scott hadn't known the famous man was related to his boss. But that still didn't explain . . .

But Mr. Hudson wasn't waiting for an answer. "A short time ago, John got wind of rumors that the girl might be kidnapped, just rumors, but a man in his position can't be too cautious, he's a target for any kook that comes along. The girl is stubborn, I admit that, and she

1

insists on going off to Europe despite the possible threat. John wants someone to accompany her for her personal safety. That's why I picked you."

"Mr. Hudson, I'm a lawyer, not a professional body-guard. There are firms that supply a need like that. Frankly, anyone they had to offer would be much better than I. Besides, you just assigned me to the Linden case, and I'm very much interested in it." Scott leaned hopefully forward in his chair.

His employer gave an exasperated sigh. "Look here, Mitchell, this is damned important! Cartwright was married to my sister. Jennifer is his only child. Her mother died when the girl was six years old. She's Cartwright's whole life. My God, if she happened to be kidnapped, he'd go out of his mind!" He leveled his eyes soberly at the young man sitting across from him. "He'd do any-thing to get her back, I'm afraid, *anything!*"

Scott sat back abruptly. "Do I understand the mean-ing behind that word . . . *anything?* You mean exactly that?"

"I do. Not only money, that's nothing to him in re-turn for his daughter, he's got plenty from his inven-tions. But you may have heard the rumors he's involved on a project for the government, something pretty damned secret and pretty damned important." Hudson tapped a stubby forefinger on his desk. "If someone got her, and they threatened enough . . . maybe torture . . . or sent back the tip of her ear, a finger, to show they mean business—that's what scares hell out of him. He's afraid, afraid of being pushed into the . . . anything."

"Secrets someone wants . . . security secrets?" Scott shifted his position uncomfortably. This was nothing he wanted to be drawn into. But how could he avoid it?

A stolid look answered him from across the desk.

"But, under the circumstances, why let her go out of the country, where it would be harder to protect her? Why doesn't she stay here? Get a bodyguard here, if she needs one?" Scott asked.

"I'll tell you the honest truth, Mitchell. It's because

Jennifer is a mighty feisty young woman! I guess her father spoiled her. I warned him over and over that that was what he was doing, from the time she was a little kid. So now she's set on going to Europe, and believe me, she's going, hell or high water! Cartwright wants someone to go with her, keep a close watch on her, see nothing happens. Can you be ready to leave Monday? That'll give you the whole weekend to get things together."

Scott straightened his long legs out in front of him while he frantically searched his mind for a way out. The idea of trailing around Europe in the wake of a spoiled brat, acting as chaperon and nursemaid to a dizzy dame, was a whole lot less than appealing.

He tried. "But, really, Mr. Hudson, a regular bodyguard, a professional, would be a lot better at giving her protection. Why me?" he protested.

"Because I know you, and because you don't look like a bodyguard, that's why! You look like a fellow she might run around with. Not some overmuscled plug-ugly with square-toed shoes—that's not what John wants. Anybody would recognize the type in a moment. You can do it. You got a white belt in judo, you speak several foreign languages. Don't argue, Mitchell!" Hudson's chins undulated with impatience.

"Black belt," Scott corrected absently. "Mr. Hudson, really, I . . ."

His employer frowned. "Remember, I told you this was an order, not a suggestion! You're going to go, just like I said you were to do—unless you choose to resign from this firm, which you'd be a damned fool to do, we both know that. You've got a future here."

He waited a moment, then began fumbling in a drawer, pulling out a thick envelope to toss on the desk in front of him.

"There you are, airline tickets, credit cards, all the rest of the things you'll need. Her father will pick up all charges. Be at the airport on time Monday, your schedule is inside with the ticket. I know you've got a current passport from that trip to South America we sent you

on in the Pomeroy case. You can certainly get all your
personal affairs wound up by the time you're to leave."

"Mr. Hudson . . ." Scott made one last valiant effort
but was quelled by a towering dark scowl on the other
man's face. "I . . . I don't even know what she looks
like. How will I know her when I see her at the airport?"

The older man lifted the envelope to shake out a snapshot to hand to Scott. "There, you ought to be able to
recognize her from this."

Scott lowered his eyes to the snapshot as he picked it
up. The picture, taken from a short distance, in color,
revealed an attractive young girl leaning against a tree,
smiling at whoever had taken the photograph. She was
not tall, but slim and nicely curved. Auburn hair, faintly tilted nose, and bright blue eyes. He studied the girl's
likeness for a moment or two. This might not turn out
to be such a tough assignment, after all, he reflected.

Looking up, he saw Mr. Hudson watching him. The
man had evidently read his thoughts. "Good-looking gal,
isn't she, Mitchell?" Then he added slowly, "She looks
gentle as a dove, but she can be a Tatar! And stubborn
as a donkey! All because her father never put his foot
down. Wanting to go to Europe at a time like this! That's
nonsense! But go she will! So go along and see nothing
happens." He shoved the drawer of the desk shut with a
thud clearly meant to signal the end of the discussion.

But as Scott rose to leave, envelope in his hand, his
boss said, "Oh, one more thing, the first part of the trip
will be spent in Venice, visiting at the home of some
Italian jet-setter, some fellow she met when he was over
here. Confidentially, Cartwright isn't happy about it, fig-
ures she's got herself wound up with a fortune hunter.
He wouldn't be too unhappy to see it break up."

Scott stiffened, half-turning from the door. "Look, Mr.
Hudson, if you chose me with the idea that I was to . . ."

His employer looked startled. "Oh, hell no, Mitchell! I
didn't meant that. Not what you're obviously thinking.
This has got to be business all the way. I suggest you

keep it that way." Then an unaccustomed grin suddenly cracked the stern face. "I wouldn't say there's any chance anyhow. Jennifer doesn't like the idea of a bodyguard one damned bit!"

2

Jennifer Cartwright boarded the plane, smiled at the stewardess, and made her way to a window seat. The jet was filling rapidly, and Jennifer settled back to watch each boarding male newcomer with a suspicious eye.

The stewardess glanced down at the manifest sheet she had in her hands and threaded her way through the tangle of passengers in the aisle to stop beside Jennifer. "I'm sorry, I neglected to check, are you Miss Cartwright?"

Jennifer glanced up. "Yes, I am."

The girl nodded. "Fine, I wanted to be certain. We are reserving the seat next to you for a . . . a Mr. Mitchell," she said after another glance down at the paper. "Thank you." There was a bright smile, and the stewardess returned to her post near the door.

So she was going to have the presence of the bodyguard beside her on the flight! It was bad enough to have him on the same plane, Jennifer reflected, frowning. That was Uncle Henry's doing, seating the man next to her.

A harried-looking woman with two small children was next to enter the plane, and behind her, a tall gaunt man with long sideburns and raddled-looking face. Oh, not that one, Jennifer prayed. He wasn't to be her keeper, was he? But he did not hesitate at her seat, moving on forward as she breathed a sigh of relief.

She cringed inwardly as a macho jock type, all muscled and thick-necked, paused for a moment to let his eyes sweep slowly over the plane, stopping at her for an instant to give her an openly admiring look that prom-

6

ised he was almost certain to corner her later with a "Say, little lady, I'm sure I know you from somewhere!"

Those bulging biceps that strained his loud sporty jacket—wouldn't he be the type her father might feel would safely guard her? Yes, he was sauntering confidently down the aisle toward her now, causing her heart to plunge. That . . . that dreadful character to be at her side for the next four weeks! Jennifer shuddered.

He hesitated at her seat row, giving her a glance that made her feel she was being systematically undressed; then the stewardess appeared at his side to murmur something, and he went on, giving Jennifer a last swift head to-toe look.

The remaining vacancies were being filled now, and still the seat beside her was empty. Maybe, Jennifer reflected, maybe her bodyguard was going to miss the plane. Perhaps there had been a mix-up in plans. She leaned back, spirits lighter. This was all ridiculous, anyhow! A bodyguard, for heaven's sake! A spark flickered angrily in the cobalt-blue eyes. It was so absurd! Demeaning.

"You'll not board that plane in New York without a protector!" her father had thundered at her, his normally quiet voice suddenly fierce, inflexible. "You promise, or you don't go! I'll . . . I'll see to that!"

Despite her protests, he was immovable. He simply folded his arms, pressed his lips together in a stubborn straight line, and shook his head. It was either agree, or miss a chance for her first glimpse of Europe. So, finally, she had reluctantly and grudgingly agreed. But how carefully Jennifer had chosen her words. Yes, she would go along with his request to not take off for Europe without a bodyguard on the same plane with her. She had given her word on that.

But she had blithely skimmed over any other specific commitment. Very well, let her assigned bird dog board the same plane. But she hadn't promised she wouldn't try to lose him the first chance she got. And she damned well would! Jennifer pursed her lips with satisfaction at the thought.

The time for departure was nearing. Still he had not
come. Jennifer relaxed against the back of her seat. She
was nearly free! She had given *her* word, hadn't she? She
had agreed to accept his presence. However, if the man
didn't come—she smiled—then it couldn't be helped, and
it wasn't her fault. But . . . hurray!

The stewardess walked up the aisle and back down it,
scanning the passengers. At Jennifer's side she halted,
looked down again at the manifest she held in her hands,
then gazed inquiringly over the empty seat.

"Mr. Mitchell, who is booked for the place next to
you. He's not . . . ah . . . here?"

"Evidently not," responded Jennifer cheerfully.

The girl frowned down at her list, hesitated, then
thanked Jennifer and moved on.

Jennifer kicked off her shoes and prepared to enjoy
her trip. In hours she would be in wonderful Italy. And
what fun it would be to see ebullient, unpredictable Mario again. He was amusing, unbelievably handsome, full
of animal spirits and charismatic charm. Her father
couldn't stand him, of course; he thought Mario was a
fortune hunter. The very fact that the first week of her
stay in Europe was to be spent with Mario and his family
had caused her father to glower and mumble under his
breath.

She sat gazing out the window. She did hope, however, that Mario understood about her visit. Jennifer
looked thoughtful. He had promised he'd read nothing
romantic into her trip. He was a darling, but she had
been honest with him, she had to be. She was not in
love with him, her meeting his family was not to be con-
strued in the wrong way, by him, or by them. Mario had
smiled down at her, those dark, bold eyes flickering with
amusement.

"Very well, *cara,* I promise . . ."

There was a sudden flurry of activity at the front of
the plane, by the entrance, a hurried conversation between a man and the stewardess. The girl nodded toward
Jennifer, and the man came down the aisle as the heavy
door of the jet swung shut.

The newcomer was tall, slim, with a wiry, rapierlike look, fair of skin but with a hard tan. His hair was a deep tawny blond. Stuffing things in his pockets as he came, he paused, gave a hurried look at Jennifer, then thumped into the seat beside her. Drawing an uneven breath, he turned to gaze at her, gray eyes suddenly darkening with an expression she couldn't read.

"Miss Cartwright?" he asked formally, balancing an attaché case on his lap.

"Mr. Mitchell, I presume?" she said crisply. Good-looking though he might be, she thought, he was still an albatross that would hamper her freedom. She bristled inside. Leave it to her father, or that wretched uncle of hers, to try to decoy her with an attractive man. It wouldn't work! This Mitchell person was still a most unwelcome bodyguard, and in no way was her plan changed about losing him along the way.

"I nearly missed the plane," he said, still sounding winded. A faint mist of perspiration beaded his forehead.

"Too bad you didn't succeed," she blurted out unintentionally, but in a barely audible voice.

He'd heard. The gray eyes snapped. "So that's the way it's going to be, is it?" he said sharply, irritably.

"Mr. Mitchell"—Jennifer spoke crisply—"I don't know if you're aware of it or not, but this was not my idea. I don't need any sort of protector, I don't want one. Sorry, but at the risk of sounding rude, I must warn you, I'm not going to be the most placid, the meekest of subjects for your vigilance. I don't like any part of the idea, and I can't pretend, even for one superficial moment, that I do."

She saw temper brewing in the tightened lines of his jaw, the muscle that jumped in his cheek. At that moment, the plane jerked, shuddered slightly, and began moving ponderously across the field.

"Miss Cartwright"—he spoke in a hard, dry voice—"I'm certain I like this assignment even less than you. I am not here by choice. I was ordered to do this by my employer, *ordered*, against my will. The alternative was losing a job I've worked hard for!"

He was eyeing her with barely controlled irritation. "You know, Miss Cartwright," he continued in that same brittle voice, "after a moment's exposure to your gentle nature and lovely disposition, I might say I can think of an unlimited number of things I'd like a whole lot more than having to trail a petulant, spoiled young woman over half Europe!"

The man turned away, drew a folded newspaper out of the attaché case, put the case away, and buried his stormy face behind the headlines.

Jennifer drew a steadying breath, pressing her lips tightly together to keep from making any retort. All right, she told herself, she'd asked for it, flailing away at him right away like that. She really hadn't meant to. What she'd honestly started to do was just be frank with him, but her banked-up irritation over her father's and Uncle Henry's high-handed arrangement, riding stubbornly over all her own wishes, had goaded her, and before she knew it, she'd exploded. Jennifer slid a covert look at him.

Apologize? After he'd called her a spoiled, petulant young woman? She sank back farther in her seat, eyelashes lowered, mouth set stubbornly.

The whine of the jet rose shrilly, the plane stirred, then began its slow heavy roll down the runway, picking up sound and speed as it went, until with a great powerful roar it lifted up into the sky, up and above the clouds, leaving Kennedy Airport far below. They were on their way to Europe.

Safety belts were loosened, and passengers relaxed back in their seats, voices could be heard, talking and laughing now. A few people rose and began to move about.

The newspaper hid much of Jennifer's seat companion's face. He flipped over one page, then another, absorbed; finally he turned to the last one, carefully scanning each column, then folded the paper neatly.

Turning to her, Scott asked, "Would you care to read the paper? Sorry I neglected to ask you before." He was coldly polite.

"No, thank you," Jennifer began almost as frostily, then halted to give him a curious look. "Mr. Mitchell, we certainly appear to find ourselves in some sort of uncomfortable contretemps. Let's be honest with each other in a situation that is embarrassing and mutually distasteful." She was extending a tentative olive branch.

"I thought we already were. Honest, I mean. You don't want me to be here. I don't want to be here." The gray eyes regarded her calmly. "That's about it. Looks like it'll be a grand four weeks, doesn't it?"

"Probably. But, I'm curious, why are you doing it? I didn't know the professional-bodyguard business was so selective, except for brawn, that you could be forced into an assignment purely to keep your job."

"I'm not a professional bodyguard," he said shortly. "I happen to be a lawyer."

Jennifer's eyes narrowed. "Oh, so that's it!" she said triumphantly. "Uncle Henry! I see it all now. I should have guessed. Uncle Henry. How dare he! I suppose you're one of the young legal geniuses he's grooming. What did he do? Threaten you?"

"I'm a member of his firm, yes," Scott said stiffly.

She eyed him frankly. "I realize Uncle Henry's law firm is supposed to be the prize plum for ambitious young men, but . . . really, Mr. Mitchell, pardon me for being so outspoken, you may well be a budding F. Lee Bailey; however, you don't strike me as your typical bodyguard type. Why in the world did Uncle Henry decide . . . ?"

"He seemed to feel I was qualified." The cool tone was still very much in evidence.

Jennifer nodded. "There's probably some truth in that; he isn't given to snap judgments concerning people. But tell me, is it true he threatened you? Did he really say you could go out the door and head for the airport . . . or the nearest employment agency?" She looked incredulous.

Scott gave a bitter laugh. "Something like that. Let's just say he made me an offer I couldn't refuse. Really, Miss Cartwright, I'm sorry I was so rude, but . . ."

"Perfectly all right. I had it coming. But I do want you to realize that this whole thing is absolutely uncalled for."

Jennifer glanced up, to see the macho-type muscle man strolling down the aisle toward her. When he caught sight of Scott talking to her, he slid a disappointed glance in her direction and walked on.

She saw Scott tense, eyes suddenly alert as they followed the man's progress down the aisle.

"Someone you know?" he queried.

Jennifer shook her head. "No. He had his eye on the seat you have, I think. Earlier."

Scott looked thoughtful, frowning. "Maybe. But I'll keep an eye on him."

She sighed. "Please don't start that. There simply isn't a problem. My father has always been overprotective, and now, after the latest—and really unfounded—rumor of a possible kidnapping, he's become almost neurotic on the subject. That's why, in order to take this plane, I had to promise to accept a bodyguard." She gave him a sudden wicked little smile. *"En garde,* then, Mr. Mitchell. From now on, you do the guarding . . . if you can."

He looked disconcerted. "If I *can?* What's that supposed to mean?"

Now her smile turned into a light laugh. "Exactly what I said—*en garde,* I shall not be the easiest quarry."

Scott stuffed the newspaper down beside him before replying. Then he turned back to Jennifer. "Do you mean you actually are going to try to evade me if you can? Lose me?"

"I do."

He shook his head, a puzzled frown wrinkling his brow. "I don't get it. Why are you telling me, then, putting me on the alert?"

"Because otherwise you might think the kidnapping threat genuine, that I've really been . . . 'snatched' is the proper term, isn't it? You'd probably fly around frantically, alerting the police, phoning my father . . ."

There was a pungent silence. The stewardess passed down the aisle, smiled at Jennifer, and went on. Quite clearly it was a woman-to-woman accolade; the girl evidently thought Scott good-looking. Maybe he was, Jennifer granted, but she could well do without him.

"I gather you don't take this kidnapping threat at all seriously, then," Scott said deliberately.

"I don't." Jennifer turned to gaze at him levelly. "Let me tell you something. Do you realize that I was never allowed to learn to ride a bicycle because a little girl who lived near us was hit by a car while riding her bike? Every one else rode. I didn't." She paused, and then added, "At twelve years of age, I got to go to a summer camp, accompanied by a . . . well, call it a governess, chaperon, whatever, to see that I didn't swim too far, get lost, or have anything else happen. Can you think what that does to a girl of that age? Do you think there was any other kid being trailed around by someone saying, 'Be careful, Jennifer'?"

And what her father didn't think of, she reflected, Uncle Henry did. Because he'd never married, he took an intense interest in helping bring her up. From clear across the country, he supervised, nagged, urged her father to clamp down on her. Now that she was twenty-one, she'd finally learned to drive a car, but only after being so immovably stubborn and outright obnoxious that her father had reluctantly given in. She'd bet he'd never told Uncle Henry.

"Well, then, even if you refuse to consider the kidnapping threat of any importance, what I'd like to know, was there really an actual rumor or not?" Scott asked curiously.

Jennifer shrugged impatiently. "Oh, I suppose so, for the hundredth time! There've been others, or my father has imagined there were, and each time he'd get that funny look in his eyes, and there'd be a spell of questioning every one of my dates about background and family in a replay of the Spanish Inquisition. As long as I can recall, I've had to struggle for every bit of freedom I've managed. Maybe that's why I object so strongly to your accompanying me."

"I can see your point of view, but . . . what if this isn't a false alarm, what if it's a genuine threat?"

"Well, it isn't. It never is. Frankly, I think my father has the ridiculous idea that I really am in danger and that Mario might somehow—and I certainly don't know how—be involved in it. I suppose you know that I've been invited to visit in Venice with Mario Forlenza's family?"

She halted to give him a sharp look. "Ah, yes, your face betrays you. I've no doubt you've been thoroughly briefed. I can almost hear Uncle Henry giving you the lowdown on Mario, calling him a fortune-hunting jetsetter. His very favorite phrase. Mario is nothing of the sort. And what did he tell you to do—be a bodyguard . . . or . . . ?" Angry blue flames began flickering in her eyes.

"Don't tell me, Mr. Mitchell, that you also have orders to break up any romance? That would account for . . . ah . . . well . . . why Uncle Henry chose you instead of some actual professional!" she said hotly.

His eyebrows snapped down angrily. "It's not why! I want that clear in your mind, Miss Cartwright. I received no such directive!" he said flatly. "I didn't want . . . correct that, please, I *still* don't want to accompany you to Europe as a bodyguard. I certainly wouldn't have come, under any circumstances, had there been such a suggestion!"

"Well, then, I withdraw that," Jennifer responded tartly. He needn't have been quite so emphatic about it, she told herself.

He slid her an indignant look. "I also want to reassure you that you're not to worry about any such idea being generated by me in the future. Your romantic life is your own affair, and mine is mine. This is a strictly business assignment. I look on it that way. I would never, under any circumstances, consider mixing romance and business. Your love life is quite safe, I assure you." He bit the last words off sharply.

Jennifer felt irritably for her shoes with a searching foot. Her seeking toe caught one shoe, and she bent to slip it on, feeling abstractedly for the other one.

Scott bent to retrieve it from under his seat, handing it to Jennifer without a word. Thanking him, she put it on and stood.

"Will you excuse me, please?" She started to pass by him. Seeing his questioning glance, she said tartly, "I'm not thinking of taking to a parachute just to lose you, Mr. Mitchell, I'm going to what is euphemistically known as the powder room. I trust you don't plan on accompanying me there!"

She went toward the rear, already regretting her unnecessary and acid comment, conscious that his face had reddened, not with embarrassment, but out-and-out irritation. She reminded herself she really mustn't allow her deep resentment at her father and Uncle Henry for making decisions over her head and ignoring her wishes to cause her to lash out at her bodyguard. *Bodyguard.* The very word startled a ripple of annoyance rising in her all over again.

"Hello, there, Jenny, what are you doing here? Silly question, isn't it?" a voice hailed her a few moments later as she was returning to her seat.

Craig Holman, survivor of four divorces and a genuine member of jet-set society, grinned up at her. He was blondly handsome in a rather jaded way, with hair so light it was almost platinum. Though beginning to show too much weight, he was still attractive and looked exactly what he was, an international playboy. Jennifer had known him several years, and though his reputation as a Don Juan was a bit steamy, she'd never felt particularly intimidated or emotionally threatened by this popular and thoroughly amusing man.

He patted the empty seat beside him. "Sit and talk to me!"

Jennifer slipped into the unoccupied space. "Only for a moment," she said. "I didn't see you."

Craig nodded. "Had my face buried in a good book, I suppose," he said cheerfully, holding up one of the more sensational best-sellers. "Improving my mind. And you, fair Jennifer, on your way to see your Italian lothario?"

She smiled. "Partly. Only the first week in Venice, then Florence and Rome. It's only for four weeks, and lucky to get that!"

up on her! What did he think, she wondered, that she could possibly escape him on the plane? She frowned.

Craig was regarding her curiously. "And who, pray, was that? The guy looks like he has designs on you. Don't tell me that you've married since I saw you last. Don't spoil my trip with such depressing news, Jennie!" he jibed, but his eyes were bright with curiosity.

"Of course not, nothing like that," Jennifer protested quickly, wondering how much to tell this international gossip.

She deliberated only a second, deciding on an airy "His name is Mitchell, works in Uncle Henry's office. He happens to be going to Italy, too. Actually, I never met him before today." That was it, neatly dividing her conscience between absolute bare truth and discreet omission. There was no reason to tell Craig; more reason not to. He'd think it was hilarious and recount it with elaborate embroidery over half the cocktail parties in Europe.

"You're not keeping something from Uncle Craig? Sure there's no little secret romance?" His eyes were on her shrewdly.

"Absolutely none. How could there be, when I've just met him?" All truth now, she reflected.

Scenting no possible provocative tidbit, Craig launched into other subjects, until Jennifer, noting food service was beginning, rose and said she really ought to be returning to her own seat.

Her traveling companion had long ago returned from his scouting trip, and as she took her place, lifted his head from a book to give her a distant nod. "I was merely checking," he said defensively.

"So I gathered," Jennifer replied. "I'm afraid that you're going to be a very busy man. That is, if you feel obliged to keep me under close observation all the time." She smiled demurely. "Remember, I warned you."

There was no response but a disgruntled sound over the top of the book.

Jennifer was conscious of his presence, aware of the stubborn set of his jaw. Was his irritation due in part to having to leave a romance behind him in the States? she wondered. Musingly, she tried to picture the type of girl he'd go around with. There was no question of his being married; Uncle Henry would never have chosen him if he were.

Well, he could go back to his romance, if any, in four weeks. Less than that if she managed to be successful in leaving him waiting for her at some street corner . . . and waiting . . . while she took a train or a plane out of his grasp. Jennifer felt she had completed her promise to her father, not to *leave* without a bodyguard.

The stewardess arrived with trays, and Scott and Jennifer ate, side by side, silently, until Scott set his fork down to say, "May I ask who that man was, the one you were talking to?"

"You may. A friend of mine, Craig Holman. And I do hope this question of yours doesn't mean you'll be quizzing all my acquaintances just as my father used to."

Now she turned to him with a questioning look in her blue eyes. "I suppose we really should come to some sort of understanding, lay out ground rules. Just how do you mean to conduct your vigilance?" She put her head to one side inquiringly. "Will you work a five-day week? Will my father pay you for overtime?" She gave him a faint smile. "I'm really quite serious, though. I'd rather like to know what protection plan you intend to follow."

"Plan?" He had again lifted his fork in preparation to continue eating, but hesitated long enough to say, "I don't know, to be truthful. Not yet. It's my first experience in the field, and I've not had much time to prepare." He ate several bites before continuing, "I should imagine it would include keeping you in view as much as possible, remaining fairly close." He didn't look particularly happy about the prospect, Jennifer noticed.

Lifting a slender eyebrow, she said, "That should certainly have clearly defined limits, I should think. It surely would rule out taking up residence, sleeping on a cot in my room."

The bit of food balanced on his fork dropped to the plate as he turned to give her a cold look. "Naturally not that!" he replied stiffly. "However, I plan to see you to your room each night, to be certain that . . ."

"To be certain I'm not sneaking out on a late date? That sounds worse than having a duenna." The gleam of a smile crinkled at the corner of her mouth, revealing a hint of a dimple that was visible only fleetingly. She really shouldn't tease him this way, Jennifer guiltily admitted to herself, but she couldn't resist it, he reacted so stuffily. "And how about Mario, if he wishes to kiss me good night? Will you stand in the offing, a watchful witness?"

Now he really was annoyed. Definitely. "Miss Cartwright, I'm going to discharge my duty the best I know how. The fact that I don't relish the job doesn't mean I won't try to carry it out to the best of my ability. I'd appreciate a little more cooperation from you, I might say!"

"Cooperation, Mr. Mitchell? I thought you understood my cooperation wasn't to be taken for granted. I told you so."

Scott glared. "You ought to realize that at any moment I may come to the decision to give up this mission and take my lumps. There are some things no job is worth." Eyeing her sarcastically, he said, "Which will not mean you won't immediately be assigned another bodyguard. I've had some experience with your uncle's stubbornness. I'm certain you'll get someone else to trail around after you. To quote a famous statement, 'You could go farther and do worse . . . and you probably will!' Just keep in mind, I don't like this one damned bit more than you do. I'm doing it only to hold a good job, but . . . it's getting so the job looks less and less inviting to me."

Jennifer stiffened at his acid comments. It was clear he meant exactly what he said. They were like two angry cats imprisoned in one small burlap bag. She stared forward for a moment, her eyes fixed unseeingly on the back of the seat ahead, her mind grasping futilely at the right words to say in reply. He was certainly correct about one thing: his replacement could be an even greater handicap. This man, despite his prickly disposition, at least looked presentable.

Scott had returned to his food. Jennifer decided to say nothing more at the moment. After the trays had been removed, she settled back to let the time trickle slowly past, her eyelids fluttered drowsily, and she drifted off to sleep.

3

A touch on her arm awakened her, and Jennifer became aware of the crackle of the public-address system.

"Sorry to disturb you, but we're over Italy now. I thought you might want to get off the plane here," Scott said as he began stuffing some papers back in his attaché case.

Jennifer yawned, then glanced at her watch in amazement. She'd been sleeping that long!

Turning her head, she met her bodyguard's half-grin. "You must have a clear conscience, you've slept almost across the entire Atlantic," he said. Then his eyebrows lifted wryly. "I suppose now the chase and the challenge begins!"

He actually was looking amused, Jennifer realized in some confusion. Somehow, she didn't quite trust this new twist of temperament. What did he have on his mind? Then she shrugged as she pulled out her purse from where it had slipped down beside her. There was no use in trying to pry the information from him, and anyhow, it didn't matter, really. She'd soon be rid of him.

"You've never been to Europe . . . Italy . . . before?" he queried as they fastened their seat belts preparatory to landing, as the warning flashed up ahead.

"No, never." Jennifer's eyes sparkled with anticipation. "Once before, I almost made it, but Uncle Henry and Father wouldn't let me go. And this time it was almost the same thing, but I gritted my teeth and hung on, to the point of being especially obnoxious and insistent." She flushed at the look on her companion's face.

21

The plane swooped down, bounced lightly, then taxied steadily down the runway. The excited voices of the other passengers filled the large cabin. Jennifer and Scott Mitchell waited patiently where they were, in their seats, as the door swung open and there was a rush of impatient travelers pressing forward to be the first ones off. Then Scott, giving a questioning look at Jennifer, said, "Shall we?"

She nodded, and they rose, gathering up belongings, Jennifer tossing her light coat over her arm. He politely reached to take it, but she shook her head. Watcher and watchee, she reminded herself silently, not two people traveling together for any other reason.

The moment they entered the airport in Rome, they were surrounded by a great clatter of sound. Voices, laughter, the roar of planes leaving and arriving, and everywhere, noise, noise, but it was exciting and stimulating. Jennifer's eyes shone with exhilaration. It was going to be marvelous, she thought, marvelous!

There was the matter of customs, of course, but it went smoothly enough. Scott looked at Jennifer, for the first time approvingly. "One suitcase? Congratulations! I thought it was customary for women to bring the contents of their entire closet with them."

"Not I," Jennifer said. "I read once that seasoned travelers learned to limit wardrobes and belongings to one piece of luggage. I thought I'd be seasoned." Her mind was only half on what she was saying, her eyes and attention caught and held by the crowds swirling about her, the excitement of being in a foreign country, the crackle of languages she couldn't understand, and over all, the faint haunting odor of roasting coffee.

Scott's voice startled her. "Say," he said urgently, "I just looked at my watch. We better hurry along, we don't have a whole lot of time to make the Venice plane."

Though he prodded her with his voice to keep moving, she found herself constantly distracted by her surroundings. He was hurrying her along with a hand touching her elbow, and when she happened to glance up at him, she was startled by the vigilant look on his face, the way his eyes kept sweeping over those around him. He really was taking his job seriously!

"See any kidnappers?" she asked teasingly.

"Probably," he said dryly. "If I find one, I'll see if I can make a deal to have him take you."

"Thanks a bunch. Meantime, you make me feel a little like the president with his Secret Service escort."

But there was little time for further talk, as they were frankly hurrying now. Yet Jennifer kept twisting her head, not wanting to miss a moment, watching the dramatic farewells of departing members of Italian families, surrounded by their emotional well-wishers, who were pressing bouquets of flowers and ribboned packages into the travelers' arms.

They were in time, barely, and when they had boarded and were momentarily expecting takeoff, they leaned back in their seats to catch their breath.

After a few moments Scott Mitchell turned to her. "Will your . . . friend be meeting the plane?"

"I presume so, someone will. We're going to his family's place somewhere in Venice."

"Does he know yet that there'll be an . . . extra?" Scott spoke uncomfortably.

"Certainly. I phoned him, of course." Jennifer gave him a quick glance up over the top of a small mirror she was using while she touched her lips lightly with lipstick. "I didn't go into complete detail, I merely said my father was apprehensive about my safety. Mario, I might add, wasn't exactly overjoyed about having a third party chaperoning the entire time, but you can count on Mario, always the gentleman. I doubt you'll be required to use the servants' entrance," she said pertly, the lightness of her voice robbing the statement of any sting.

Putting the mirror away, she looked around the plane and out the window before turning back. "You know, I can't go on calling you Mr. Mitchell if we are going to be thrown together for four solid weeks. I don't suppose we should advertise to the whole world why you're traveling with me, and being on such formal terms does just that. I'm Jennifer, Jennie, whatever, and you're . . . ?"

"Scott. You're probably right about that. Jennifer." He grinned at her.

"And"—she sighed—"I've said all I have to say about not wanting you along. I'll not go on repeating it. You've made your side equally clear. Let's call it a truce."

He looked at her doubtfully as she raised long golden lashes over guileless eyes. "I don't know that I quite trust you," he said slowly. "You look too damned innocent. Truce? Does this mean you won't give me any problems, won't try to ditch me at the first opportunity?"

"It does not," she said wickedly. "I mean only that I shall attempt to be more civilized, more polite in my conversations with you."

The doors of the plane were shut, and soon they were up and away, north toward Venice. The sky was an incredible blue, filled with soft feathery puffs of clouds.

"Not to get into a touchy subject again," Scott said, "but though you've made it clear you don't believe in the kidnapping rumor, what if it turns out you're wrong and you do actually get kidnapped? How about your father's role in this? If you are tortured, or threatened with torture, and he knows it . . . what's that going to do to him?"

"He'd feel terrible . . . as he would if I'd been hit by a car while I was riding a bike as a kid. Or if this plane"— her eyes ranged about the interior of the cabin—"if this plane should crash, there would be the same reaction of grief. One simply can't go on half-living in fear of what *could* happen!"

Scott gave her a flat look. "Those comparisons are not the same at all. In a kidnapping, you might still be alive, it would still be possible to save you . . . if certain requests were filled. Your father could be faced with a terrifying choice—not for money . . . but . . ."

"Oh, so that's it!" Jennifer pounced triumphantly. "So Father would be pressured into giving up details, secret ones, of the project he heads!" Her voice was clearly exasperated. "Don't tell me where you got that idea. That's Uncle Henry! I can just hear him. That's *his* idea. My father would die, I hope he would let me die, before he would reveal one . . . one equation."

"You uncle could be right," Scott persisted stubbornly. "It's a terrible decision for a parent to be forced to make."

"It won't happen. But that's Uncle Henry. His self-appointed task of trying to tell Father what I should do, or deciding it for himself, drives me up the wall! Ooh!" She shuddered with irritation. "Why doesn't Uncle Henry leave my life alone!"

Scott gave an appraising glance at her face, gone faintly pink, and decided to leave the matter for now, so he leaned back in his seat and closed his eyes.

Jennifer slid a covert look at the strong profile with its straight nose and firm chin line. He really did take all this seriously. His query about Craig, the ridiculous cloak-and-dagger way he had acted in the airport in Rome. No doubt that was a mere taste of things to come. She sighed. Four more weeks of this? Four weeks that should have been gay and lighthearted, now to be overshadowed by the constant suspicion and surveillance by the man next to her. And Mario—how was he going to react to a male chaperon?

There was no other solution: she must rid herself of Scott as soon as possible. The sooner the better. The only decision left was when and how.

She hadn't long to mull over that, for the trip was brief, and the plane was soon circling over the Marco Polo Airport outside of Venice. Scott opened his eyes in a way that made her think he hadn't been asleep at all, but merely withdrawing from the conversation.

From where Jennifer sat, she had a glimpse of the sea below as they began their descent. The water was sparkling like a million diamonds in the sunlight, the effect dazzling to the eyes. Her heart quickened in anticipation. Venice had long been the place she had dreamed of, and now she was here!

Again came the routine of buckled seat belts, the landing, the disembarking. At first Jennifer couldn't see Mario anywhere in the crowd clustering about the incoming travelers. She and Scott pressed slowly through passengers and greeters, making their way toward the baggage area, when suddenly Mario was there, outrageously handsome face, dark bold eyes, and she was enveloped in a pair of strong arms.

"Carissima!" Mario, pulling back to look down at her with affection, lifted one of her hands to kiss it in dramatic continental fashion.

"At last you have come to my country! My life begins today!" Mario appeared oblivious of the silent Scott standing patiently a few feet away.

"Mario," Jennifer protested weakly as the Italian continued to hold her close, eyes openly adoring as he gazed at her, disconcerting her, "Mario, this is . . ." She twisted, drawing slightly away, turning toward Scott. "This is Scott Mitchell, my . . . well, my bodyguard."

What else could she call him? she thought perplexedly. After all, Mario knew about him. "Scott, this is Mario Forlenza."

"Pleased," said Mario, extending a casual hand, which Scott took as he returned the greeting.

Jennifer noticed that there was a covert sizing-up between the two of them, and how Mario, the civil niceties having been observed, was quick to turn back to her with an intimate smile.

"Very well, now, *cara mia,* we shall take a gondola to my home. Not a *motoscafo,* what you call a motorboat, but for you, today, you must enter my beloved city in the ancient and traditional manner. First, however, the luggage."

But Scott had already stepped to the area a few steps away and was receiving their suitcases. A porter took them, and after a short order in Italian from Mario, was headed for the water's edge.

Mario turned to look back over his shoulder. "Mr. Mitchell, will you accompany us, please?"

The question was almost academic, Jennifer realized, for Scott was already following, keeping a discreet few steps behind as they started for the boat landing.

Jennifer suddenly halted to gaze about her, every sense

responding to the magic wonder of Venice, the bobbing boats, the heady scent of sea air mingling with that seemingly ever-present one of roasting coffee, the quick voices and light laughter about her.

And just a few steps ahead lay the long slender black gondola, with its faint tilt of the prow, brass hardware shining in the sun, opulent velvet cushions on the seats. The gondolier, dressed in white, with a red sash, wearing the famous flat straw hat with a crimson ribbon, lifted chocolate-brown eyes, momentarily bold and admiring, as he flashed a look at her before instantly resuming a stolid disinterested stare straight ahead.

Mario stepped forward to help Jennifer into the gondola, taking the seat beside her as Scott settled into place in front of them. A nod by Mario to the gondolier, and without a word of direction the man swung the craft slowly away from the docking area, heading toward Venice.

For a long, long moment Jennifer was raptly silent, filling her eyes with the distant outlines of buildings and towers as the gondola moved quietly through the water.

Mario bent close to her, and she became aware of the faint light scent of shaving lotion. "My dear Jennifer, your cheeks are pink and shining, your eyes are like stars. That tells me you are excited and aroused by your first glimpse of my city." His fingers, tanned and slender, folded over her hand.

She had a fleeting disturbed feeling that Mario was a bit more demonstrative than she had remembered him, but the thought was eclipsed by the spell that captured her now. Forgotten was Mario by her side, Scott, everything and everyone but the slender spires and clock towers, the great rounded cupolas pushing up out of the magic city ahead.

As they drew nearer, Jennifer could see arched bridges, then delicate buildings, rising on either side, ocher-colored and seemingly spun out of pale brown sugar, with closed arched doorways only inches above the flowing water going past them.

But she was abruptly startled out of her reverie by the

harsh roar of a motorboat sweeping past and on down
the Grand Canal, sending up a wake of bumping waves
that rocked the gondola.

"That," sighed Mario regretfully, "is the curse of modern Venice, the *motoscafo,* to which we all surrender
sooner or later. The gondola is charming and leisurely,
but many times one must hurry."

"It does rather disturb the peaceful mood," Jennifer
said as the intruding boat disappeared around a curve in
the canal ahead.

"And, I'm afraid, is contributing to the decay and
destruction by undermining the foundations of Venice,
once Queen of the Adriatic." Mario leaned close to touch
her ear with a kiss.

Jennifer shifted uneasily against the velvet cushion
behind her. She wasn't accustomed to such open displays
of affection, and it wasn't quite what she'd expected from
Mario. Too, she was acutely conscious of people passing
in other gondolas, of the gondolier poised behind and
slightly above them on his small platform, and she was
relieved that Scott had not witnessed the romantic display
of intimacy. Certainly she thought Mario was fully aware
of the basis for her visit—friendship, and no hint of
anything else. She must reinforce that at the first opportunity; this wasn't quite the time or place.

A stolid wide-bottomed boat chugged slowly past, its
sides lined with sitting passengers. A group of green-
uniformed schoolchildren waved, and Jennifer smiled
and waved back.

"That's our Venetian version of your city bus,"
Mario said, "the *vaporetto,* very cheap, runs often. As
you know, we have no automobiles in Venice, transpor-
tation is by foot or by boat. And I, Jennifer," he said
grandly, a smile curving the firm mouth, "shall be your
personal tour guide. When we reach the *palazzo,* it is
customary for you to tip your guide properly, in this
case . . . a kiss?" He spoke gravely, but his dark eyes
flickered lights deep within. "All guides must be tipped,
one way or another. Otherwise . . . who knows what will
happen next time?"

Jennifer, flustered, moved her glance away to exclaim over a small boat filled with flowers, pulling up to an open flower market on the edge of the canal. Mario was charming and fun, she reflected, but in the States he definitely hadn't been quite this impetuous. And she wasn't ready for it, not yet, and she wasn't sure it was the relationship she'd ever want with Mario. Whichever way, she felt uncomfortable at the moment.

Ahead, rows of boats were halted, motorboats that had passed them, the *vaporetto,* pulsing impatiently. Jennifer's eyes flew open wide in astonishment. "A traffic light!"

Mario nodded. "Of course, and much traffic, my love. Though we do not have cars, our morning and evening rush hours . . ." He lifted a shoulder in an expressive Latin shrug. *"Fantastico!* We even have police boats. And need them!"

Their gondola moved forward with the rest when the light on the other side of the canal changed to green.

They passed under arched bridges and past countless waterways that twisted and led to unseen destinations, lending a mysterious quality to the place. Jennifer found herself reflecting that there was a strange exquisite melancholy over everything, not a feeling that made one sad or depressed, but it was as if she were looking into the long-ago past, haunting and half-lost in the passing of time. There was an air of gentle decay about many of the buildings, their plaster scarred and faded. But gay red-and-white poles for mooring boats stuck out of the water, giving a rakish look to the scene.

Now their gondola began slipping from the main part of the canal, to one side, to draw up before an impressive-looking two-story building studded with balconies and arches, white against the deep coffee-cream facade.

Jennifer turned to Mario questioningly, and he answered her look with a nod. "This is my home, Jennifer," he said almost formally, "and I bid you welcome to it. My mother waits to greet you. She did not come to the plane, wishing to give us this little time for a private meeting. Though, I must say . . ." He slanted a wry look at Scott's back. "My sister returns shortly."

Mario stepped out onto a small platform to aid Jennifer in alighting. Her mind's eye was still filled with the dignified air of the building she was about to enter, but there was decay evident here, too, bricks and mortar showing bare beneath the plaster.

"The luggage will be taken care of, Mr. Mitchell, come along, please." There wasn't quite the tone of an employer addressing a servant in Mario's voice, but it didn't miss by much, Jennifer observed.

But Scott, if he noticed or minded, gave no sign. He was reserved, proper, and followed them inside after Mario had drawn a key from his jacket to unlock the heavily carved door.

The dim entry hall was round, with a marble floor that had as its center a huge many-shaded marble star radiating points to the walls. Jennifer had the fleeting impression of darkly shaded tapestries and deep red velvet draperies.

A door at one side opened, and a gray-haired woman came across the floor toward Jennifer, both hands outstretched.

"My dear Miss Cartwright, welcome to Palazzo Forlenza. You forgive, please, if I do not speak the English well. I understand, but I fear when I talk, I mistake often."

Jennifer received the impression of gray as she greeted the slight figure before her, soft gray hair drawn gently back into a Grecian knot, gray frock of some finely spun material, gray kid shoes. Only the eyes meeting hers were different; they were Mario's, dark, expressive, but without his bold daring. Her manner was slightly constrained but gracious.

"You speak English, though, and I, I'm afraid, know no Italian," Jennifer said regretfully. "I hope I shall learn some, it's such a beautiful language."

"Do not allow Mario to teach you Venetian dialect." The older woman mockingly scolded her son with a loving glance. "It is not true Italian." Then her eyes lifted slowly to focus over Jennifer's shoulder.

"This is Mr. Mitchell, who accompanies Jennifer," Mario said.

Jennifer wondered if Mario had explained beforehand about Scott's role.

His mother answered the question in Jennifer's mind by saying, "Welcome, Mr. Mitchell, I understand you are here for . . ." She halted, frowning, clearly searching for the word; then her patrician face lightened. "Ah, to protect, is it not? It is to hope no occasion does arrive."

Before Scott could do more than politely acknowledge the introduction, a thin, elderly, bent-shouldered woman clad in a maid's black uniform appeared in one of the doorways.

She ducked her head at her mistress. *"Contessa,"* she began, following the word with a short phrase in Italian.

Contessa? Jennifer did know that word. Then, if Mario's mother was a countess . . . was Mario a count? She slid a glance toward him, and he must have understood her unasked question, for he gave her a wry smile, shrugged, and nodded.

"Your rooms, they are ready," the countess said. "Emilia will show you the way."

Jennifer and Scott mounted the wide stairway leading up to a second floor, following slowly behind the barely moving maid. The frail woman led them down a hall, past many closed doors, to stop before one that was massively carved with lions and twining vines.

She pushed it open, and Jennifer stepped inside, to halt just past the threshold and turned inquiringly to the servant woman. The maid nodded, confirming that it was indeed Jennifer's room, then stepped back and closed the door.

"I wondered if you'd make it. So you finally escaped the prison walls. Good for you! Parole, or lifetime pardon? Is your father going to allow you to be free at last?"

Jennifer shrugged. "It's a step."

Craig nodded his approval. "When you spoke of this projected trip, I wondered what your chances were. You're far too handsome a gal to be kept forever under lock and key the way you have been."

They chatted casually for several moments about mutual friends. She couldn't help smiling at his wickedly gossiping comments made in his animated way. There was something irrepressibly amusing in his lighthearted manner; he never appeared depressed, never dour, seemingly without a care. He appeared to exist comfortably on obscure but unlimited means. She wondered how he managed. His enemies—and he had some, usually the target of his gossip—claimed his money came from divorce settlements.

Lifting his eyebrows dramatically at Jennifer, Craig relayed the news that he was embarking on a new romance with a lovely English girl of irreproachable family and wealth.

"Tons of money, really," Craig related happily. "But it's love this time, it really is! Stop smiling, Jennie," he chided. "I know you've heard that before, but this time I mean it! She's vacationing in Italy . . . so I am, too."

At that moment, the edge of Jennifer's vision was caught by a stirring from the seat she shared up ahead. Her bodyguard's dark blond head rose, and he turned to peer down the aisle. She wasn't visible, she knew, hidden by a large man two seats ahead, who was now standing, leaning over his chair to talk to someone in back of him.

Good! That Mitchell person might as well get used to the realization that he wasn't going to supervise every single step she made. Turning back to Craig, she went on with their conversation.

A few minutes later, she became aware that a tall figure was standing by her seat, eyeing her for a long silent second before moving on. So he'd decided to check

4

For a long moment after the door shut, Jennifer stood still, looking about her, almost too delighted and enchanted to move. The furniture was slender and Venetian in style, touched with gold leaf, the marble floor partially hidden by a rich red Persian rug, worn but still exuberantly glowing with color. The walls were decorated with fragile, pale, Fragonard-like frescoes that had, sadly, begun to surrender to dampness and age, though they still retained their pastel delicacy.

It was, Jennifer decided, exactly like a room roped off with a velvet cord in a museum, something kept almost miraculously intact, if a bit faded, from the long-ago luxurious past.

She walked slowly over to the long French windows that opened onto a balcony overlooking the canal. The sun was shimmering on the water, faintly gilding the houses across the way. Standing out on the balcony, gazing over the city, Jennifer felt her heart quicken. It was altogether so exciting and romantic, a fairy-tale land. She wouldn't have missed it for anything. Even having to tolerate Scott's overwary supervision wasn't enough to spoil it for her.

There was only one faintly disturbing impression that crept unbidden into the corner of her mind. The contessa. Charming, aristocratic, gracious . . . but . . . but what? Jennifer frowned, biting thoughtfully at her underlip. Hadn't there been the faintest of shadows in the woman's soft dark eyes?

Jennifer's thoughts were disrupted by the sound of

men's voices outside her bedroom door. Cocking her
head to one side, she listened. Mario and . . . yes, Scott.
Not arguing, not exactly, but it sounded like rather force-
ful conversation on both sides. What was wrong? She
heard her name being mentioned.

Spinning about, she hurried to the door to throw it
open. The two men were standing in the hall, a few steps
beyond her room, Scott's luggage at his feet, determined
lines running down the edges of his mouth. Mario appeared quite calm, but dark fires smoldered deep in his
eyes.

They both turned. "I'm afraid I've become a problem,"
Scott remarked dryly. "The room adjoining yours is not
being occupied, so I have requested that I be given it. The
palazzo is large, and the room in the other wing, though
very nice and certainly comfortable, is too far away to
give you adequate protection."

There was a tight look to Mario's lips. "And I, un-
derstandably enough, am not enthusiastic, and no offense
meant, Mr. Mitchell. Jennifer is quite safe here, as I
have assured you. Quite safe. However . . ."—Mario was
reluctant, that was easy to see, but he surrendered, not
completely graciously—"it will be as you wish, if it is all
right with you, Jennifer."

"Why . . . yes, yes, I suppose so," she replied, because
there seemed no other comfortable response. And Mario
wasn't happy about the situation, not at all, she realized.
What was it, she wondered, the suggestion of possible
intimacy? Surely not! He understood Scott's role. And
Scott? It was impossible to tell by looking at him. He
looked calm . . . and immovable.

Jennifer felt a flicker of annoyance. This was all so
silly! It was what came of her father's stubborn in-
sistence on her having a bodyguard.

Mario gave her the trace of a bow and said stiffly,
"Of course, Jennifer, if you will feel safer." He turned back
toward Scott. "Very well, Mr. Mitchell, in here, please."

Shoving open the door, Mario stood back while Scott,
picking up his luggage, began moving into the room

next to Jennifer's. Mario, silent, watched him, with color reddening his olive skin along the high cheekbones.

When the door to Scott's room had closed, Mario turned to Jennifer. "Sorry if I sounded rude, *cara,* but I felt this change quite unnecessary, and, quite frankly, it is beginning to look as if our Mr. Mitchell is going to be . . . what you Americans call a pain in the neck."

But his stern look melted as he took her hand. "Just be certain to lock the door that joins the two rooms. I had really expected your bodyguard was going to be a gruff, husky, middle-aged man, possibly with the need of a shave, wearing a powder-blue suit. Not"—he tilted a sardonic eyebrow at her—"not someone about my age, and what is commonly thought of as attractive, or at least I imagine women find him so."

Jennifer glanced over at the closed door. "I hadn't a choice, you know, not about having a bodyguard, nor which one was picked. That was taken out of my hands. Scott Mitchell works for my uncle, so I suppose that's why he was selected."

Mario gave her hand a gentle squeeze. "Very well, my love. But you shall see Venice in spite of our determined shadow. Perhaps some evenings we can evade him and spend the time alone somewhere, without his knowledge or presence." His eyes met hers meaningfully.

"Perhaps." Jennifer neatly sidestepped any promise. This new and more ardent Mario disconcerted her a bit. Then she started and said, "Mario, you are a count? You don't use the title? I had no idea. It surprised me."

"It's not important, really. Here in Venice, where we've lived for generations, it is still used by some, by servants and shopkeepers, by some friends here and there, but . . . really"—his eyes shuttered momentarily, impossible to read—"it doesn't mean the same as it once did."

Then his mood abruptly changed. "Now, promise to come downstairs to the salon shortly. My sister will be arriving from Paris within the hour, and we shall have an *aperitivo* or some tea." Mario sighed. "Mr. Mitchell, too, I presume."

After he left, Jennifer shut the door and stood leaning

against it for several moments, thinking. This was certainly going to be a little more complicated than she had ever imagined. Scott was clearly taking his job too seriously. And Mario. Jennifer lifted her hand to tousle her hair absently. Oh, dear, she reflected, Mario was turning out to be a problem, all right. He was going to take a bit of firm managing.

She smoothed down the hair she had unconsciously ruffled, the motion as preoccupied and bemused as the tousling. Men could sometimes be such problems!

What had caused Mario to change so? She was certain he had been different in the States. Oh, he'd been affectionate, but only in a cheerful, teasing way. Now, she thought uncomfortably, it was all changed. She thought she detected an intense, almost purposeful display of affection. It was strange and somehow disturbing.

When she'd first mentioned her proposed trip abroad, Mario had immediately insisted she be sure to see Venice, and invited her to stay at his family's residence. She'd almost reluctantly agreed, after she thought he understood. But apparently he hadn't, or he was ignoring all agreements.

Walking slowly over to the French windows, Jennifer stepped outside once again onto the balcony to stare down at the passing string of boats, all sizes, all kinds. Lifting her eyes, she looked out over the buildings to where a church tower was chiming the hours. But she was registering none of these things, only her own inner thoughts.

Abruptly there was a metallic click of a latch, and the French windows nearby swung open. Scott stepped out onto the same balcony.

"Planning to jump in? It's one way to ditch me, but I don't think I'd recommend it. Water looks a little . . . um, murky." He made a face. Then, turning to gaze down the Grand Canal, at the bridges and labyrinthine small waterways, he said, "Seriously, it all seems unreal here, doesn't it? We get off a plane and step into bygone centuries. This place and New York are in different worlds.

Take that man over there, strolling across the cobblestone street."

She peered over the water to the other side, where a man carrying a large package was making his way awkwardly over to a store, where he disappeared inside. Jennifer looked puzzled. She looked back over her shoulder at Scott. "What about him?"

"He was walking, not running, not dodging a car or a bus. Not even looking either way. Can you picture what would happen if they lifted the guy from here, to set him right down in the heart of New York? You'd hear cabbies yelling, brakes screaming, or . . . maybe the sound of an ambulance."

She nodded slowly, but her thoughts had turned in another direction. "Scott, really, must you take this assignment so literally? It wasn't necessary at all for you to make such a big thing about changing your room. It does seem a little distrustful of the Forlenzas. I'm certain Mario must have felt that."

He grinned, his face lighting up, gray eyes crinkling. "I'm sure your friend didn't like it at all! But I was sent to take care of you, prevent anything from happening. I will. You certainly take no precautions. When I got on the plane, you didn't even ask me for any sort of identification. You might have been fooled right from the start. I *could* be a kidnapper, you know."

She gave him a sarcastic eye. "Really. About as authentic a kidnapper as the kidnapping rumor. It's turned out it wasn't necessary to quiz you, anyway, hasn't it?" Jennifer turned back to look at the water. "Just don't ride the protection role too hard, please."

Scott was silent for a moment. Jennifer would have loved to turn around and see what his face was registering—stubbornness, probably—but she refrained.

"This isn't my idea of a great time, either, you might consider," he said at last, his voice sharpening. "It's four weeks' waste of my time, when I could be doing other things. But your Uncle Henry is a stickler for what he calls 'seeing the job through.' All I can say is that I hope he isn't going to consider this my vacation for this year." He sounded definitely disgruntled now. "I could inform him otherwise. It's not my idea of a vacation, certainly. It's bad enough to be set bodyguarding without having to justify every move and action."

Jennifer opened her lips to reply, then closed them firmly. It was futile to argue. It might not be his idea of a vacation. Well, he ought to know by now that he wasn't adding to hers.

She contented herself with turning, giving him a cool nod, and going back into her room, closing the shutters firmly behind her.

Jennifer opened her suitcase and for the next few minutes busied herself with hanging up her clothes in the heavy old wooden wardrobe that occupied one corner of the room, its heavily carved doors swung open wide. Changing from her traveling clothes, she showered quickly in the enormous old-fashioned bathroom and returned to select a simple pale-blue frock with a gold link belt to wear down to the salon.

Slipping the dress over her head, she wriggled into it, smoothing it over her hips, then stood back from the mirror to peer appraisingly. Demure and modest, the dress was. She gave her reflection a wry smile. Just the sort of thing a girl would choose to wear when meeting the family of a special young man.

Jennifer frowned. That was the problem. Picking up a brush, she began brushing her hair until the reddish sheen glowed, as she tried to consider how to tactfully handle the situation. Somehow she sensed that hot fires burned under the sophisticated charm of this new Mario, and once they were unleashed, might not be easy to get under control again.

One last quick inventory of herself in the mirror, then she went out into the hall, shutting her door softly behind her, giving a stealthy look at the room next to hers. Scott wasn't really a necessary adjunct to her every step.

At the foot of the stairs she halted, hesitating. Upon hearing voices from an open door, she crossed the marble floor and entered a room rich in color, turned golden and bronze by the last rays of the setting sun. Here, too, the warm glow of Persian rugs, and here, too, the signs of fraying and age.

Mario and his mother were seated on a heavily carved tapestried sofa, and in the center of the room, coat thrown back loosely from slim shoulders, stood a young woman who could only be Mario's sister. The same dark, high coloring was there, the flashing eyes, hers rimmed with incredible long black lashes. She resembled nothing so much as a fashion model from the cover of a magazine.

"Cara!" Mario bounded from the sofa as he glimpsed Jennifer in the doorway, and crossed the room to take her hand, drawing her forward. "Come, I wish you to meet my sister, Angelina."

The girl turned liquid velvet eyes to gaze at Jennifer with frank curiosity that was in no way rude, but showing appraisal nevertheless.

She's judging me, seeing if I'm all right, Jennifer thought uncomfortably.

But the girl broke into a sudden shining smile. Coming forward, she held out a slender hand. "Charmed, Jennifer, we've heard so many nice things about you from Mario. How good of you to come visit us!"

Thank heaven she speaks English, Jennifer reflected. Then she voiced that relief aloud. "Thank you, and I must admit you all put me to shame, speaking my language so well, and I speaking nothing at all of yours except, perhaps, *Arrivederci Roma* and *ciao*," she said regretfully.

"Ah-ha! Then I shall teach you at once to say *ti amo* . . . now repeat . . . *ti amo!*" Mario said boldly.

His mother clucked at him in a scolding way, and his sister shook a finger at him. "How naughty of you," the girl said. "Mario, one keeps such intimate lessons for intimate moments. She will say 'I love you' when you deserve it, and only if you do!" Turning to Jennifer, she said, "And I'm not certain he does!" Her smile robbed her comment of anything but teasing family affection.

Abruptly Angelina's eyes lifted, the long silky lashes sweeping wide. Mario and Jennifer swung around, to see

Scott standing in the doorway, not entering, simply
letting his eyes run quickly around the room.

"Come in, Mr. Mitchell," Mario said stiffly, "we shall
be serving *aperitivi* shortly."

"I was merely ascertaining that Miss Cartwright was
present." Scott's tone was almost as stiff. "She wasn't in
her room when I knocked."

"Well, she is here, here and safe. My sister, Angelina
Forlenza, Mr. Mitchell." Mario's voice made it clear he
was accepting the situation of an ever-present duenna, if
not liking it.

Jennifer was startled by the almost magnetic charm
that suddenly radiated from the girl. And . . . Scott?
Jennifer watched as he stepped forward to take Angelina's
outstretched hand. There was a definite response, a reaction, however carefully controlled, in his face.

"*Piacere,*" he murmured courteously, adding another
phrase or two in Italian.

"Oh, but you speak Italian!" the girl said delightedly,
dark eyes sparkling.

Scott gave a deprecating smile and shrug. "*Un po,*
I'm not all that fluent. I only wish I were."

Jennifer was startled. This was a different Scott. The one
she was all too familiar with was the faintly disgruntled,
typically Madison Avenue young-business man type, assigned to a project he found unappealing—to say the
least. She eyed him curiously. This Scott was quite another person, somehow urbane and charming. Maybe, she
reflected, it's because he's responding to a beautiful girl,
not dealing with a stubborn client.

An elderly man clad in the dull black of servant's
clothes wheeled in a tray laden with fragile-looking crystal glasses and decanters. Bowing briefly, he left the
room. Mario pulled the tray in front of him and looked
up over it.

"I've vermouth and Campari to offer. Also, Mr.
Mitchell, scotch, if you'd prefer that. The vermouth,
Jennifer, is our own north-of-Italy variety, Punt e Mes,
which you may find a bit astringent to the tongue, an

acquired taste, perhaps, but quite favored here. There is also tea, if one wishes."

Jennifer tilted her head to one side thoughtfully, trying to decide, then decided upon the Punt e Mes, as did Mario and Angelina. Scott settled for a scotch and soda.

The countess contented herself with tea, smilingly touching a pale hand on the gray dress. "My doctor allows me the luxury of an *aperitivo* no more. For my health's sake, it is better I not use."

Jennifer cautiously tilted the small etched crystal glass to let a few drops touch her tongue. It was bitter, she decided, yes, and at the same time, sweet, too. Odd and somehow pleasing.

She sat back in her chair, holding her glass by its fragile stem, and gazed about the room. The atmosphere was growing more relaxed, she thought, a lot more than it had been, becoming almost friendly between Scott and Mario as time flowed past lazily. They were using each other's first names now, and Mario's prickly attitude toward Jennifer's bodyguard seemed noticeably diminished.

And it was easy to see that Scott was enjoying the presence of the gay, vivacious, but intensely feminine Angelina. Jennifer couldn't blame him; she found the girl delightful, too. Angelina had an incandescent personality, and was drawn to Scott, too, that was evident, with that bright attentive air she bestowed on everything he said, her quick soft laugh bubbling up at comments that passed between them in low voices.

Maybe, thought Jennifer slyly, it wouldn't be so difficult to lose Scott, after all. Here she'd made all kinds of complicated, secretive plans in her mind on exactly how to go about it, going into considerable mental detail on the best timing for her scheme. Now she wondered if he'd even notice.

She slanted another look at the two sitting side by side on the sofa opposite, their cocktail glasses seemingly half-forgotten on the large carved table in front of them. Abruptly, and a little ridiculously, Jennifer felt a bit miffed. Not that she minded Scott's interest in Mario's sister, she told herself firmly and somewhat irritably, it wasn't that at all. But she'd been building up such wonderful mental visions of Scott's stunned, frustrated reactions when he found she'd vanished without a trace.

Dinner that evening was served by candlelight in the formal dining room, the two elderly servants moving soft-footed and slowly behind the table, wearing white gloves, serving the food, removing the plates with unobtrusive efficiency, which seemed a little strange when compared to their tortoiselike pace.

Jennifer scarcely noticed what she was eating, though her taste buds told her it was good, but she was so entranced by Mario's tales of ancient Venice, of the doges, the intrigues, the feared rule of the ten inquisitors and their power to punish, that she found herself bending forward wide-eyed, her fork barely lifted from her plate. The Forlenzas, she learned, had lived in this very *palazzo,* generation after generation, since the latter part of the 1600's.

Angelina smiled at Jennifer's rapt expression. "What a true romantic you are, Jennifer. I can't resist telling you that the famous, or infamous, Lord Byron once sat in the very chair where you now sit."

Jennifer turned fascinated eyes toward Mario's sister, who was looking at her with an indulgent, affectionate expression. "Here? I know that's a silly thing to say, but it's a little startling to me. At home, we have a myriad of places George Washington is supposed to have slept, but I've never been in one. And I cross an ocean to spend my first evening in the same room where my favorite poet once was. But . . . do you mind my asking the circumstances? Or is it rude to inquire?"

"Not at all. Byron loved Venice, which he rather grandly called the 'master mold of Nature's heavenly hand.' He spent a lot of his short life here, and my ancestors, who were fond of poetry and poets, invited him to dine. Once. Then they learned of his notorious debaucheries and his affair with the Countess Teresa Guiccioli, and, the story goes, he was never invited again." Angelina turned her beautiful eyes toward Scott. "Byron really was quiet a naughty man, if the tales whispered to this day in Venice are true, and my forebears were fore-runners of Victorian morality, I think."

Mario leaned toward Jennifer. "After dinner, my dear, I should very much like to expose you to the most romantic experience of our romantic city, a gondola ride down the Grand Canal under the moon, with a singing gondolier at the oar. Daytime may be pleasant, interest-ing, but nighttime . . ." He gave her an intimate look from those dark eyes.

Jennifer caught a sudden alert glance from Scott. She had the feeling that the romantic gondola ride was not going to be unchaperoned.

"But perhaps you're too tired," Mario said, concern abruptly appearing in his voice, "the jet lag. If you'd rath-er wait until another night?"

Jennifer shook her head so sharply that her auburn hair flipped across her cheek. She pushed it back, saying, "I should hope not! I would love to. I don't even know if I'm tired, or what time it is back in the States, maybe it's four in the morning, I don't want to miss one single mo-ment. I can always sleep."

Mario laughed and reached over to squeeze her hand gently. "Then we shall go, we shall indeed!"

"Is this a trip that requires an invitation?" Angelina was asking her brother, half in fun, half serious. "Or . . . would you prefer that you and Jennifer . . ." She gave him a knowing quirk of the eyebrow.

Mario sighed. "Come along. I have a feeling that we won't be alone anyhow, the two of us." He looked over at Scott. "Right or wrong, Mitchell?"

Scott smiled agreeably. "Oh . . . right . . . right. I'm like Jennifer—I wouldn't miss it for anything. It'll be the prime example of how you can mix business and pleasure. So, you, too, Angelina?"

"Of course . . . to quote two famous people, 'I wouldn't miss it!' "

As they walked down the long hall after dinner, Jennifer halted before a painting hanging on the marble wall.

"It's Venice, isn't it? St. Mark's Square? I've seen other pictures of the square, but none so beautiful as this."

Mario's mother moved up to stand beside Jennifer. "It is indeed Venice. Canaletto does this one." She smiled at the girl. "I'm happy you like. So do I!"

Mario said, "We shall be seeing this exact scene tonight. Not a modern version, exactly this, except for the clothes the people are wearing. Canaletto painted it when he was a young man. He did many of Venice, but this is my favorite. Remember, this was done in the 1700's —think of that when you see the place tonight." He reached forward to put a lean tanned finger on the painting. "And this, this small café or coffeehouse, is Caffè Florian, where we shall have coffee this evening."

Jennifer stared at the arcades that arched over the place Mario had spoken of. She felt someone move up close, and realized Scott was also at her shoulder, his breath warm on her hair, his chest touching her as he leaned forward to see. Instinctively she recoiled, as if she had touched or been touched by something hot. She turned her head, glancing at him as he pulled back, seemingly not noticing her reaction.

"A true Canaletto . . . you're fortunate, Mario," Scott was saying admiringly. "Beautiful . . . and valuable."

"Indeed it is. Once we had two . . ." Then Mario's voice halted abruptly, as if he felt he had said more than he'd planned.

Jennifer might have wondered why, but she was still wrestling with her uncomfortable response to Scott. She actually disliked the man that much, did she? She tried testing her feelings on the matter, and decided it wasn't that, but that it was all based on her resentment of having him foisted on her against her will—of having him underfoot for the entire trip. If . . . if indeed he had to be. She lowered her eyes, keeping the thought to herself, all the more set on eluding him the first moment possible.

"If you are ready, Jennifer, we can take a leisurely ride on the canal now. I might suggest you take along a sweater or light coat. It may turn cool a bit later." Mario placed an affectionate hand on her arm. *"Mamma, e tu?"*

The countess shook her head. "Not I, my dears," she said smilingly, "for the young people, the night air . . . good, maybe, but for us, the old, it makes the bones to ache and stiffen."

Jennifer went hurrying up the stairs, followed by footsteps behind her. She didn't have to turn to know it was Scott. Going directly to her room without turning to make any sort of comment to him, she closed the door and went to the dressing table to pull out a drawer. Taking out a sweater, she held it up to her dress. Good, it would contrast, not clash, the darker blue against the pale blue of her frock. A coat seemed unnecessary; the air coming in through the open windows seemed soft, with the feel of September warmth.

As she opened the door to leave her room, she found Scott, hands plunged into his jacket pockets, whistling almost soundlessly under his breath, gazing at the tapestries on the wall, as casual and relaxed as she'd ever seen him since he got on the plane.

"Ready?" he inquired blandly, his attention only partly on her, partly still on a perusal of the tapestry, where a deer seemed to be evading a trio of hunters.

"I am," she retorted, her response coming out a bit more tartly than she'd expected.

He turned, eyebrows lifting, but when he spoke, it was only to say, "You know, Jennifer, I was wrong about one thing."

"Yes?"

"I believe I said I thought this four weeks was going to be a waste of my time. . . . Well, I must say I was wrong." His eyes flicked toward the end of the hall, where Angelina stood waiting for them, smiling. "Oh, I was completely wrong. Now it looks like something I'm going to enjoy."

Jennifer bit down on a retort that anything that would change his attitude would be welcome, and said only, "Good."

She was aware he gave her a swift sideways glance,

but she walked on ahead down the hall to join Angelina, Scott following.

The Italian girl was wearing a feathery white shawl draped over her shoulders, and it formed a striking contrast to the glowing olive skin and dark hair.

"Everyone set?" Mario opened a door and came out to join them.

Down the stairs they went, the four of them, across the marble foyer, to the door. Outside, the waters of the canal, dark and mysterious, shimmered where the shaft of light shone from inside the *palazzo*. When the door shut, small sprinkles of light from a heavy wall sconce splattered over the water.

The gondola was waiting; it might have been the same as the one they had come in but a few hours ago. Jennifer couldn't tell, for darkness shadowed the face of the gondolier.

As before, she and Mario sat in the back, against the velvet cushions. And, as before, Scott sat in front, but this time Angelina was beside him, her lovely profile silhouetted flickeringly by the wavering wall light.

A jerk of Mario's head, a lift of his hand, and the gondolier knew they were ready, starting the slender craft away from the *palazzo*. Above them, the stars were brilliant in the night sky; the entire canal bobbed with lights on the many moving boats.

As they poled past winding side canals, Jennifer leaned forward to gaze down them, the dark waters flowing between houses, brooding and mysterious. Small glowing lights over some of the doorways shed only pale circles of brightness, making the scene even more eerie.

She turned to Mario. "It's strange how real the past seems here. I saw a shadowy figure in a small boat just now, rowing without a sound down that small canal back there, and I had the queerest feeling it was a servant on his way to betray his master to the ten inquisitors, as you told us they sometimes did." Jennifer shivered slightly, to her uneasy surprise.

"Illusion, my darling Jennifer. Venice is all a city of illusion." Mario twined her fingers in his with gentle affection. "Once there was nothing here but saltwater marshes. Somehow, magically perhaps, a city was wrested from it . . . but now"—his voice grew bitter—"what man takes from the sea, the sea will repossess, and Venice is slowly sinking. One day . . ." he turned to look at the moonlit buildings. "One day, it will all be gone."

Abruptly his tone changed. "How rude of me to depress you with such talk. I mean only to show you the beauty and romance of my city, and instead I'm shedding great tears of regret and sorrow!" He said it lightly, smiling down at her, the passing lights catching his strong features, but Jennifer was aware the lightness was only in his voice. He cared deeply for his city, she realized, and somehow it drew her to him a little more. But, she reflected almost regretfully, it was a feeling of sympathy, of empathy and appreciation, not of love.

Angelina's silvery laughter rose from the seats up in front, followed by a low murmur from Scott. He was certainly a different person with the Italian beauty than he had ever been with her, Jennifer realized once again, remembering the glum, taciturn companion of her air trip.

The black waters, slowly moving, were silvered with the moonlight, shattered with wobbly reflections of the bridges as the gondola passed underneath arches. Sometimes the air was filled with the shrill whistle of the *vaporetti* chugging past, and sometimes almost all sound disappeared except the slow slap of an oar in the water as they moved along.

Then, from in back of her, Jennifer heard the achingly sweet sound of the gondolier's voice, singing, the words strange and unintelligible to her, but it didn't matter; all that mattered was the clear lyrical voice singing softly and passionately in the moonlight as they floated along. She felt sudden tears come to her eyes from the sheer beauty of the moment.

Between songs, Jennifer turned to Mario, wresting her eyes away from the ghostly silhouettes of the old *palazzi* on either side. "I envy you, Mario. This is the most beautiful, romantic place I've ever seen in my entire life."

His arm slipped around in back of her, his hand tightening on her shoulder. "Romantic enough to make you want to spend the rest of your life here . . . with me?" he asked softly.

Jennifer caught her breath in dismay. This was completely ridiculous! How many times had she seen Mario? A half-dozen times in the States. And today. He couldn't possibly be serious. And yet, somehow . . . she knew he was. Oh, dear, this would never do! She bit nervously at her lip. He mustn't be led into thinking she might . . . she might . . .

"*Cara,* you haven't answered me." His voice was no less ardent for being barely audible.

"But," she stammered, shifting uneasily in the pillow-backed chair, "I told you, months ago, Mario, when I said I'd come for a visit . . . I . . ." she began helplessly.

"Ah, but that was in your country. Now you are in Italy, where everyone is in love," he said teasingly but with a sober undertone.

"I really can't . . . I mean . . ." Her voice dwindled and halted as he lifted her hand, turning it over gently to press a light kiss on her palm. She really mustn't allow him to go on misunderstanding this way, she prodded herself nervously.

"Please, Mario, I like you very much, but that's not the same as love. I warned you . . . I'm not . . . well, just don't be serious . . . please," she begged unhappily, gently withdrawing her hand from his.

"Very well, then, for now I refrain," he said, clearly making an effort at lightness, "but I don't give up. I wait my chance. Tell me one thing, though, it's not because of . . . ?" He nodded briefly at Scott's back.

At that, Jennifer shook her head positively. "Of course not! I've only know him since he got on the plane. I'd never seen him before then. You know that, Mario," she scolded lightly.

Scott? Never! That opinionated, aloof . . . aloof . . . Her lips tightened. Never!

"Then, I warn you, I shall do all I can to change your mind, my darling Jennifer!" Mario said, capturing her hand once more.

"But if I don't, will you understand, please? Change, I mean?" she asked pleadingly.

"If I'm refused, then I shall undoubtedly plunge to my death into the waters of the canal, just like one of Lord Byron's jilted loves, who threw herself in despair from the balcony of a *palazzo!*" His voice held the trace of a smile.

Perhaps Mario wasn't serious, not really, maybe this was part of the Italian romantic charm at work. Jennifer sighed inside herself. She wished she could believe that was all it was. He had sounded a little too intense for joking. But why? Why was he suddenly and unexpectedly ardent? Surely, she reflected, surely he couldn't have fallen in love with her so quickly. Love has to have time to take root and grow, it doesn't happen overnight or in a few days—that was all in fairy tales.

She was relieved that the gondolier picked this moment to again begin singing. She was saved from having to make other comments to Mario in answer to possible questions from him. It was disconcerting, she felt, that she seemed to be helplessly drawn into an emotional involvement in spite of her protests.

The gondola slid to a silent halt at the landing based at the foot of a large square surrounded by brightly lit buildings. Crowds of people strolled about, along the water's edge and over nearby bridges, but many sauntered toward the large inner quadrangle ahead.

"Very well, Jennifer, we get out here, and now on to Caffè Florian for coffee, part of tonight's guided tour!" Mario was smiling down at her as he helped her to step from the gently bobbing boat up onto the platform.

Angelina and Scott followed, Scott's hand on the girl's elbow even after they had left the small craft, Jennifer noticed. He seemed to be more swayed by the romantic air of Italy than she was herself, Jennifer thought dryly.

Then she had no time for further thought about Scott and what appeared to be his budding romance, for her eyes were being caught and dazzled by the sights about her. Lifting her head, her steps slowing, Jennifer gazed up at a statue poised on the top of a slender tall pillar.

"I've seen that somewhere, I know. It's a lion, isn't it, but one with wings . . . a griffin?" she asked, turning to question Mario.

"It's the winged lion of Venice, the famous symbol of St. Mark, put there hundreds of years ago." Mario grinned as he added, "You'll see it everywhere. Not only on buildings, stamped on prayerbooks, but also on ashtrays and fountain pens and every tourist gadget imaginable. I'm afraid our city's emblem has gone commercial."

To her right lay a three-winged marble palace, a fantasia of pink and white, like frozen lace, with delicate arches and balconies.

"And that's the Palace of the Doges, isn't it?" she asked, almost breathless.

"It is indeed," Mario said. "Tomorrow we shall return to visit it. Ahead of you, on your right, also, is the famous Basilica of St. Mark. We Venetians, without the slightest bit of prejudice, mind you, believe St. Mark's is one of the world's most magnificent churches." He laughed down at her. "We could say it is the *most* magnificent, but we are modest."

"Ah, what do I hear?" Angelina's voice broke in. "Do I actually hear my brother claiming modesty as one of his traits? Does he claim to be humble, Jennifer? Then . . . caution! This precedes a trap!"

"I am warned!" Jennifer answered, with but half her mind, however—the rest of it was enchanted by the spectacle before her, around her, the whole world sparkling tonight.

She took a long quivering breath as they turned from the arched and columned portals, the oriental domes of the basilica, to make their way across St. Mark's Square. Suddenly she halted, unthinkingly grasping Mario's arm.

"It's your picture, the Canaletto, Mario! That café under the arches, the square, it's exactly the same. The people, no, but everything else. I can't believe it! It could

have been painted today, tonight, and it would be just
like your picture!"

For some reason she was almost singing inside, her
heart beating mysteriously light and high. *Why?* She had
no idea, except that she found herself smiling, not even
aware of it until Mario spoke.

He had quickly placed his hand over hers, imprisoning
it. "Ah, see, the magic is working! You're happy, are you
not? The next step will be when you suddenly dis-
cover something deep in your heart." The dark eyes gazing down at her were flashing and bold.

They were approaching Caffè Florian, with its dia-
mond-shaped marble walk under the arches, and began
threading their way past the small tables outside, where
people sat drinking coffee.

Inside the café, it was crowded, but a nod from Mario
brought an elegantly dressed waiter scurrying to his side.
Bowing, the man murmured, *"Si, il conte Forlenza, imme-
diatamente!"* There was noticeable deference and respect
in his tone.

They were led past other Venetians and tourists to a red
velvet banquette against the wall, Mario insisting that Jennifer sit facing the café patrons so she could gaze out
into the square and watch the ever-changing parade of
passersby.

"Please do," murmured Angelina. "I come here so often. You must have the seat of honor." Turning to Scott,
she gave him her radiant smile. "You and I, my dear
Scott, shall sit below the salt, facing our betters. Next
time, however, we shall sit there, and they here!"

"I don't believe I've ever seen so many people out
strolling in an evening!" Jennifer leaned forward slightly
to gaze out the tall slender windows. "Where are they
all going? Where have they been?"

"Nowhere," Mario replied. "It's what we call the evening *passeggiata,* the promenade, one walks to see and be
seen, one of our customs."

As dishes of *cassata* were set before them, Jennifer
sighed dreamily as she regarded the rich dessert with its
layers of cream, pistachio, chocolate, and fruit. "And I

can see whipped cream, too! Oh, dear, here goes a half-dozen unneeded pounds!"

She caught Mario's admiring look that somehow sent the pink stealing up her cheeks, and she turned her eyes quickly away to pick up her spoon, and began eating industriously.

Angelina and Scott were talking, and the girl was telling him of the famous people of the past who had sipped coffee here. Jennifer leaned forward to listen.

"Casanova spent his time here between his many romances, the most powerful doges met here, often to discuss unofficial business. Even your painter, Whistler, came."

"Umm, interesting," Scott said, but his voice sounded so preoccupied that Jennifer turned her head abruptly, to find he was staring fixedly into the gold-framed mirror behind her. Then he lowered his eyes to say quietly, "Don't be obvious about it, Jennifer, but do you know the man who is sitting two tables down, on our side of the room, facing us? He just came in. Dark jacket, longish hair, thin face."

Jennifer obediently allowed her gaze to roam casually over the room, past the statues of cupids, the paintings on the wall, by the man in question, then to the dark-edged windows before returning her attention to the waiting Scott.

"No, I don't . . . think so. Unless . . . unless . . ." She frowned, those at the table suddenly gone still. There was something nibbling at the edge of her mind, something she couldn't quite identify. What was it? Where was it? The airport? The plane? Yes . . . that struck a responsive note. That must be it . . . the plane. Those long sideburns looked faintly familiar. But she wasn't positive, not really.

"He might be one of the passengers from the plane, Scott. I think so, and I'm not all that positive, but now that I think of it, he may have got on the plane when I did on the West Coast; then, when I took another plane in New York, the one we took, Scott"—she looked at her bodyguard and nodded slowly—"I think he

changed there, too, at the same time. There was a man
with long sideburns on both flights, but I didn't even
realize that until now."

She hesitated, then added, "I'm only guessing, you understand. He's not exactly a memorable type, and there
were so many passengers." She attempted to sound light
and faintly amused by his question, yet her heart was
bumping uncomfortably behind her ribs. But that, she
decided, was caused by the tight lines of Scott's face and
the eyes gone suddenly hard and alert.

"Have you ever seen him before—I don't mean on the
plane or here, I mean *before?*" he prodded.

"No, I don't think so. I just don't know." What was
all this about? Wasn't Scott just imagining something?

But he cut ruthlessly into her thoughts. "He was on the
plane, all right. He changed in Rome when we did. I
watched to see who was going where we went. I wonder
what he's doing here?"

Suddenly the little bubble of fear that was forming inside her burst, and she relaxed against the seat. "I presume he's possibly wondering the same thing about us,"
she said lightly. "A tourist, probably. Wondering where
he saw us before . . . if he's even noticed."

"He has, I caught him watching when I happened to
glance into the mirror," Scott said bluntly. "Who knew
your itinerary ahead of time?"

"Oh, Scott, I can't possibly say. A number of people,
I suppose. All the family, and by that I mean my father
and uncle, and some of my friends. Why?"

"I wonder if that guy knew, found out somehow."
Scott seemed to be thinking aloud rather than addressing
her or anyone else at the table.

"Pardon me, but may I break in, if the 'alarums and
excursions' are over for the moment?" Mario was regarding Jennifer and Scott curiously, his eyes moving from
one to the other. "Could I ask what's going on? Are you
serious, Scott, about being suspicious of what looks to
me to be a rather harmless-looking individual?"

"I was sent along to be suspicious of anyone or anything that seems at all unusual. Every future action has

to have a beginning somewhere, by someone. I'd just like to stop it before it starts."

Mario was leaning back now against the banquette, eyeing Scott thoughtfully. "Then you are serious! I'm amazed, though, that you could see anything clearly in these mirrors, so cloudy with age."

"Clearly enough." Scott looked stubborn.

"This is just what I predicted would happen if my father and Uncle Henry insisted on being so overprotective and so alarmed about some silly kidnap theory. I'm sorry, Scott," Jennifer apologized ruefully, "but you really don't need to spend your time looking around corners and suspecting every person you feel looks questionable for one reason or another."

Scott gave her a quick look that had irritated impatience stapled all over it. So, all right, she told herself, it wasn't his idea to come along as her unwilling bodyguard. He'd certainly made that clear. Well, it wasn't hers, either. She had to stem the sudden desire to tell him so again, but she smiled instead, a sweet condescending smile that she was wickedly pleased to note reddened his face. Now they were even.

Angelina raised her incredible lashes to look questioningly at Jennifer. "Aren't you afraid, then . . . don't you really believe there's a threat? I'm not sure I'd be as brave."

"You would if you knew my father and uncle as well as I do." Jennifer laughed. "When I was in high school, my father kept me in the house, *in the house,* mind you, for one whole month, just because a child had been kidnapped a thousand miles away and one night he found the lock on the back gate forced. It turned out that it was someone trying to steal his car, but that didn't matter. I couldn't go to school, I couldn't go to parties. And that was just one of a number of occasions the same kind of thing happened. Now do you see why I'm not at all concerned this time?"

"All the same, it would worry me, if I were you," Angelina said. "Luckily, I'm not, for I've never been known for my bravery."

"When it comes to flirting, however, there you get an A, as the Americans say. Watch it, Scott, Angelina is a wicked coquette!" Mario grinned affectionately at his sister.

She made an impudent face back at Mario as Scott was saying, "Too late. You should have warned me sooner!"

Jennifer decided they'd all outflanked Scott with their comments and he was being reluctantly convinced that his suspicions were unfounded. So, apparently, the immediate crisis was over concerning the stranger, who was now greedily spooning his ice cream. Scott gradually lost his tense expression, and conversation began floating idly into more frivolous channels.

They dawdled over coffee as the evening grew late. Jennifer, keyed up with the excitement of the trip, the haunting charm of Venice, the spirited conversation about her, was not aware of being weary until she suddenly and unexpectedly yawned.

"Oh, I'm sorry," she apologized hurriedly to the amused faces of the other three. "That happened without my knowing it, really. I'm not tired, though," she declared staunchly.

"My dear Jennifer, it's home for you." Mario glanced at his wristwatch. "It's nearly midnight, so it must be many hours since you had any sleep." He signaled the waiter.

"It's all right, Mario," Jennifer protested weakly. "I slept on the plane coming over, but . . . maybe it's the famous jet lag. I don't want to break up a pleasant evening for everyone."

But the others were clearly preparing to go, so Jennifer rose, too. As they left Caffè Florian, she noticed that the seat where the man had been was empty. He had gone, so Scott was wrong, after all. Had he any plans of following, he certainly wouldn't have left before they did.

The crowds still strolling about had lessened only slightly as the four of them made their way across the square and over to the boat landing, where the gondola was awaiting them.

There were fewer boats and fewer lights as the gondola began its slow journey back along the canal. As they went gliding through the dark waters, the gondolier began singing once more, but softly now. Mario again slipped his arm around Jennifer. This time she did not pull away, being too relaxed, too drowsy, to protest. Her eyelids fluttered shut to the sound of singing and the soft slap of water against the buildings along the canal.

A sudden muffled bump startled her awake, to find they had arrived at the *palazzo,* the gondola nudging the small landing platform. Jennifer lifted her head drowsily, only then realizing she'd been resting it on Mario's shoulder. The thought disturbed her; she wanted to dampen down, not promote any such show of intimacy, lest it unfairly encourage Mario. Jennifer regretted she'd allowed herself to drift off to sleep while his arm was around her.

Scott and Angelina had risen to their feet and were stepping onto the landing. Jennifer quickly followed, to wait for Mario to speed the gondolier on his way and then unlock the door into the *palazzo.*

They entered quietly, crossing the foyer and going up the stairs, where Angelina left them to go to her room after a whispered good night. Mario escorted Jennifer down the hall, Scott walking a discreet few steps behind.

At her door, Mario halted, to look meaningfully at the bodyguard, who eyed them both, grinned, and politely turned his back.

Instinctively Jennifer withdrew slightly as Mario gathered her into his arms, bending to kiss her. "I . . . I . . ." she whispered protestingly, but her lips were stilled by a romantically expert kiss.

"Good night, Jennifer, I promise you a lovely tomorrow," Mario said softly as he lifted his head. "Dream of me tonight, please. A pleasant dream!"

He opened the door, and she went in, flustered, but she managed to turn and say good night to both of the men, then closed the door, stinging from the appraising, amused look in Scott's eyes as he had turned. The man was impossible!

Undressing quickly, Jennifer slipped into the soft, pale-green chiffon nightgown, then into bed as fast as she could. She was dead, absolutely exhausted. Yawning once or twice, she bunched her pillow, flipped off her light, and the room was scarcely dark before she was asleep.

But not for long. Jennifer turned over in bed, nuzzled at her pillow, pulled the blanket up close to her chin, and tried desperately to slip back into sleep. Her mind stirred irritably. Why was she awake when she was so bone weary? Maybe that was why. Maybe she was too tired to rest well. Puckering her brow, she frowned into the dark. This was absurd! *Why* couldn't she go back to sleep?

After several more futile minutes, she rolled over to look at the hands of her travel clock, shining in the dark. Three o'clock!

She'd been asleep only a couple of hours. Sighing, she tossed restlessly about until finally she gave up, and piling both pillows behind her, sat up in bed. She could see the moonlight edging the heavy velvet curtains pulled over the French windows with their small glass panes. She stared at the silvery frame for a moment, then, with a quick shove, pushed back the covers, feeling on the floor for her slippers, and tiptoed across the carpet. Very well, she told herself, if she couldn't sleep, she didn't have to waste her precious time in Venice lying there in bed fretting. Outside that window lay the glamour of this fascinating city, and she could feast her eyes on it for a while.

The dampness of early morning lent a faintly musty smell to the room. It was sad, Jennifer reflected, to see this room, this *palazzo*, the entire city for that matter, slowly slipping into decay.

Even the windows to the balcony were affected by the moist morning air, for she had to jerk on the handles a bit sharply to get them open. She hesitated a moment, wondering if the faint sound had carried. But she heard no one stirring, nor making signs of having heard, so she stepped outside into the clear cool moonlight.

She shivered a little, realizing she should have put on her robe, but she didn't bother, too entranced by the moon shining on the ghostly white dome of a church some distance down the canal.

From somewhere in the distance came the sound of singing, faint, but so poignant, so nostalgic, it was like a hand tightening about her heart. Moving to the railing of the balcony, she stood there, mesmerized, hardly daring to breathe lest the distant music be lost to her ears.

The magic moment was shattered by the barely audible click of a latch behind her. Jennifer swung around sharply, her heart leaping into her throat.

A shadowy figure stepped forward into the moonlight. Scott, wearing a robe belted about him, stood there, his tawny blond hair tousled, face grim in the light, hands shoved hard on his hips.

"What in all bloody hell are you doing out here at this time of night?" he hissed belligerently.

"It isn't night, it's morning!" she hissed back, all too aware of her nearly transparent gown that revealed more than it hid. Perhaps, if she stood still, she thought, he wouldn't notice.

"I couldn't sleep," she whispered.

"Well, I could. If I had the chance!" Scott snapped.

What a lousy disposition the man had, she told herself. Leave it to Uncle Henry to pick an impossible oaf.

"Then why aren't you sleeping?" Jennifer made her voice airy and cool. "No one's stopping you."

"I'm not sleeping because I heard the sound of something being opened. How the hell was I to know if someone was getting into your room or not? If it was only your Latin boyfriend, I wouldn't care. But . . . I couldn't chance it."

Jennifer drew in her breath with a sharp angry sound. Not for one moment was she going to stand out here and listen to such brazen nonsense. Of all the impudence!

"I'm going back to bed," she whispered haughtily, and started back to her room.

"Jennifer . . ." His voice halted her for a second, and she turned impatiently. "Jennifer, I have a suggestion to make. You really better not wear that . . . that outfit you've got on around that hot-blooded guy who's pursuing you. I don't think you can run that fast."

She glared at him, then, face burning, stalked inside. The windows that she latched behind her didn't close fast enough to shut out the sound of a muffled amused laugh.

5

Jennifer woke next morning to the muted sound of boat traffic outside the window. Throwing back the covers, she padded across the Persian rug to the French windows to throw them open to the morning sun. She took a deep trembling breath. It was still there! That almost miragelike city rising out of the water! She had the strange feeling that it would have completely vanished in the night, like a dream.

A knock at the door made her turn around, hesitant, startled. Then she pursed her lips; surely it couldn't be that oaf from next door, checking on her, seeing if she had been kidnapped in the night? Didn't he ever relax his supervision? This was getting beyond the absurd. Imagine, following her out onto the balcony like an anxious bird dog . . . and then making those snide comments. She certainly wasn't going to go to the door!

But the knock came again, so she pattered over silently to stand by the door and say, "Yes? Who is it, please?" She couldn't allow him to disturb the entire household.

"Signorina?" It was a thin, elderly voice.

Jennifer pulled the door open a trifle and looked out at the ancient stooped woman servant who stood there, a tray beside her on a small folding table. She looked at Jennifer, then nodded at the tray. *"Caffè, signorina."*

Oh dear, Jennifer thought, the poor dear doesn't understand English, and I don't know how to say anything to her. So she contented herself with nodding vigorously and smiling as the woman lifted the tray, carrying it into the room to a round marble-topped table by the window. Turning, she gave Jennifer a rheumatic little bow and left the room.

There was a tiny white china pot of coffee and a small pitcher of hot milk, a hot crunchy roll, and some marmalade. Jennifer pulled up a chair and found herself famished. Apparently one ate in one's room in the morning . . . or perhaps this was merely the forerunner of a complete breakfast later, not just the token continental one, she reflected.

Sitting there, warmed by the morning sunlight, pouring the hot milk into her cup of coffee, Jennifer was glad of the respite, of not having to face Mario or Scott right away. She had problems with both of them, and she had some serious thinking to do without delay.

Last night she had been so startled by Mario's unexpected romantic kiss that she'd not had the time or opportunity for reaction; it had come too quickly. Sipping at her coffee, she contemplated the situation. Here was Mario, as charming and as entertaining as he had been on his visit to the States, but there was something almost determined about his ardor and his fervid assault, however romantic, upon her emotions, that puzzled and disconcerted her.

And she could think of no answer to why he had changed so radically. In the meantime, she told herself, she must be terribly cautious about her attitude toward him, not to encourage him unintentionally, lest he misunderstand. At the very least, it would be unfair. That made her sit back in her chair, cradling the cup in her hand. It would be unfair only if she had no intention of ever being serious about him in the future.

Well, how did she feel about that? She frowned, her mind circling about, trying to give her the truth. To her surprise, she discovered she was shaking her head slowly from side to side without realizing it. Mario was charming, she liked him very much indeed, but love? No, not love, not now and, she realized a little regretfully, not ever. Which did present a problem. She had to start being firmer, without being rude. After all, she was a guest, here on his invitation. And that, of course, was the problem. Quite possibly she shouldn't have come.

Jennifer heard the sharp click of the French window next door . . . unlatching. And *that* man! She scowled, setting her cup down in its saucer so sharply that it rattled. Until one week from now, she realized, she couldn't very well lose Scott unless she also made a sudden and unannounced departure from Mario and his family.

Belatedly she grabbed her robe off the chair nearby and wrapped it quickly around her. Scott might appear in the open French windows, to look in on her, playing his Sherlock Holmes role.

He did not, so when Jennifer finished her coffee and roll, she dusted the crumbs that had splattered about on the table into her plate, then rose to get dressed.

Angelina was starting to descend the stairway just as Jennifer reached the top landing. The Italian girl looked as beautifully groomed, certainly as stunning, in her casual shirt and slacks, as she had last night. Together they walked down the stairs.

"You will find additional breakfast in the dining room, Jennifer." Angelina smiled at the slim American girl. "Mario and I both studied in England and picked up the English breakfast habits, much to my mother's dismay. She shudders at the thought of such things as eggs and kippers in the morning."

"Is that where you learned English? Both you and Mario speak it so well, without any accent, really, except a slight English one," Jennifer said.

Angelina nodded. "My father sent us off to be 'properly educated,' he said. We spent holidays in France for the same reason."

"Your father . . . he is . . . ?" Jennifer inquired hesitantly.

"He died three years ago," Angelina said as they entered the dining room, where sun poured in through windows thrown wide to a balcony.

There was no one else present as they took seats at the long table. Angelina motioned toward a long buffet, where silver-covered dishes waited.

"A civilized breakfast, Jennifer. I can't imagine how I existed on rolls and coffee all those years." As they rose to help themselves, Angelina carefully placed a small amount of scrambled eggs on her plate, looking wistfully at the portion. "I do suppose I really shouldn't be eating anything but fruit, though. The photographer will be furious with me when I return."

At Jennifer's questioning expression, Angelina explained. "The fashion photographer. I do modeling. And, oh, dear, how the camera does exaggerate even the fraction of an extra pound!"

"But you're so very thin, Angelina."

"Ah, how kind. I wish you were the photographer. For he will growl and say, 'What have you been eating down there in that heathen country of yours . . . pasta, I suppose? You are gross!'" Angelina gazed longingly at a piece of toast, then resolutely turned away.

"I hope you don't mind waiting on yourself at breakfast, Jennifer. Emilia and Beppo are busy with other things, so we take care of our own serving at this meal." Angelina shook her head. "Oh, the poor old dears really should retire, but they plead to stay on, they have no other home, and we—" She made a rueful face—"we cannot afford other servants. So we all manage together . . . more or less."

Jennifer carefully buttered her toast. So that was what accounted for the wistful decay of this once grand mansion. Money. Or the lack of it.

"Good morning, Scott!" Angelina's bright voice lifted Jennifer's head.

He certainly didn't lose much time in picking up her trail, Jennifer reflected, turning to give him a brief good morning. She felt a small guilty pleasure in noticing his eyes still looked a bit drowsy and his hair stuck up stubbornly in one tiny tuft in back, as if he hadn't quite had time to completely subdue it.

"Good morning, Angelina; good morning, Jennifer. I trust you both slept well after our pleasant evening," Scott said smoothly. Only the merest hint in his eyes as they moved toward Jennifer revealed that his comment included a veiled reference to last night on the balcony.

Jennifer quickly dropped her glance, to pick up her fork and vigorously stalk a small bit of egg around her plate. The moonlight had been clear and bright, her filmy gown all too translucent. The thought brought blood to her face, and she kept her head down in hope he wouldn't be aware she had caught his comment and the implication.

But there was little need for Jennifer to worry; he and Angelina were already talking animatedly as he filled his plate and brought it back to the table, apparently continuing some conversation they had begun.

"No, I don't work this week or next," Angelina was saying to him. "Mostly it's on assignment, anyhow. Fashion photography is a sometime thing at best."

"Is most of your work done in Paris?" Jennifer asked. "I mean, where the high-fashion designers are?"

"For the most part, yes. But some in Rome, and I've just finished a whole series of pictures in the Greek isles," Angelina said. "So I'm free for now. Thank heaven. I shouldn't have wanted to miss your visit. We're going to have lovely times!"

Though she was looking at Jennifer, somehow the object of her comment didn't seem to be Jennifer. Not entirely, anyhow. For the Italian girl slid an amused glance in Scott's direction.

She laughed, a joyous gurgle of sound. "Here I'm saying 'we,' but I must remember Mario—he may have special plans for you, Jennifer. Alone."

"I hate being the proverbial wet blanket or skeleton at the feast, but I'm afraid those times alone will not be entirely alone," Scott said cheerfully.

"What's that I hear? Don't be too certain, friend Scott!" Mario strode into the room, stopping by Jennifer's chair to lift her hand, kissing it, his eyes seeking hers with a warm, intimate look.

Scott's polite grin at Mario's comment seemed a bit grim at the edges. Darn Uncle Henry, Jennifer thought, not for the first time, why did he pick such an obedient, dogged, one-track mind as the one sitting across the table from her? The only freedom she was going to have on this entire trip was whatever she could wrest away from herself by losing Scott as soon as possible. Unfortunately, not until next week. Meantime, she'd simply have to accept his presence as an unavoidable burden.

One quick look at Mario's face, however, made her realize that he had other plans—ones in which Scott quite clearly didn't figure. But the handsome Italian skipped comment on the subject and began discussing what Jennifer might wish to see first.

"Everything!" Jennifer said gleefully. "The Doge's Palace, St. Mark's. If you don't mind, I'd like to cram every single waking moment full of . . . well, everything!"

"Done and done!" Mario was nodding in agreement. "And tomorrow or the next day, if the weather remains fair, we'll go to the Lido, to the beach, the place people call the most fashionable bit of sand and water in Italy."

The gondola was waiting for them as they stepped out the door. "It's the same gondola and gondolier we had yesterday, isn't it?" Jennifer asked as she settled back in the chair, leaning forward slightly as Mario insisted on placing velvet pillows behind her. Scott and Angelina took their usual places in the chairs in front.

"You're quite right," Mario said. "It's our gondola, belongs to the family, for generations, really. I'm not certain how much longer, however. It, like the *palazzo*, is ancient and in need of repair. Beppo's grandson, Paolo, is the gondolier when we need him."

Mario's voice had a strain of regret when he spoke of the gondola, a strain he attempted to cover by adding, "But one hates to abandon what is truly the most romantic way to travel. Legend says the crescent moon dropped out of the sky one night to shelter a pair of lovers, and that's the reason for the shape of the gondola, a crescent moon."

He took Jennifer's hand in his. "Jennifer," he said in a quiet voice that would not reach as far as the front seats, "please consider spending your entire four weeks here with me in Venice. It's so very little time at best. It could be very important to both of us . . . a period for our hearts to speak."

"But, Mario," she protested, aware she was about to say the same thing all over again, that she thought he understood, but his fingers were touching lightly on her lips, stilling her voice.

"Please, *cara*, don't tell me no, not yet. Let me hope. Let's have today and tomorrow, the next day, and perhaps by then you won't leave, won't want to leave. We'll send Scott back to the States, and I shall guard you with my life, my beloved Jennifer!" He smiled down at her, but the dark eyes were earnest.

Jennifer squirmed uneasily against the cushion behind her. This was really too much! Mario was like a spirited animal running with the bit in his mouth, reins loose, unstoppable. For the first time, she felt actually troubled about him. It wasn't so easy now to write all this off as Italian romanticism. There was something just a shade too purposeful about it.

But Mario was nodding toward the two in front. "See, didn't I tell you that Venice brings out romance in us all?"

Scott was bending close to Angelina, his dark blond head, still with that silly errant tuft of hair, almost touching hers. Angelina's richly alive face was turned slightly toward him, eyes meeting his, a sparkling smile on her lips. He was saying something to her in a low voice, and she was nodding. Jennifer watched them speculatively.

So what! What did she care about what he did? Not one single bit, but after all, he *had* accepted the job of being her bodyguard. Jennifer blinked suddenly, a bit appalled at her abrupt reaction. How childish and silly she was being. Why wasn't she absolutely delighted at having Scott distracted by Angelina? It certainly gave *her* more freedom. Jennifer toyed with the question for a second, then cast it from her mind with an inward scowl, refusing to allow it any more time in her thoughts.

The gondola floated smoothly down the canal. Jennifer eyed the buildings on either side with interest that turned into curiosity. "Mario"—she turned back to face him—"I keep looking, and I don't see any. I haven't seen one in Venice. Venetian blinds, I mean. The windows are all either shuttered or barred, and I see nothing but draperies or curtains . . . and not one venetian blind."

Mario laughed, and Angelina, having overheard, twisted around, giving a delicious little chuckle. "Jennifer," she said, "I hate to disappoint you, but the real story has very little glamour. I understand when the blinds were first made, they were bound with a strong canvas known as *rasse,* or venetian. So called, I suppose, because the material was made here, but made here no longer. But the name stuck in spite of"—she shrugged—"in spite of no venetian blinds in Venice. Dull little story, I'm afraid." She lifted an eyebrow and smiled at Jennifer. "Don't trust Mario to give you the background on anything; he can't resist a romantic explanation." She made a face at him.

"Impossible girl, my sister," Mario said cheerfully. "My parents should have considered dropping her into the canal at birth."

But the conversation was ended by the bumping of the gondola gently against the landing where they had moored at the base of St. Mark's Square the night before. As they stepped up onto the dock, Jennifer gazed about her. How very different it all looked by daylight, she observed. Not less beautiful, no, the starchy white lacelike front of the Doge's Palace was as dazzling, but last night's shadows edging the bright lights had lent a special mystic spell.

From room to room, inside the palace, the four of them wandered, heads craning back to stare up at the paintings on the ceilings, gazing at the portraits of the doges, stern and patrician in their ancient costumes. Jennifer found she was often catching her breath and holding it momentarily in sheer wonder.

"Now, here," Mario said, "is the door that no one wished to see. Remember I told you about the feared ten inquisitors? The Room of the Black Door has the Lion's Mouth, that dreadful letter box where messages were left, secretly and unsigned, betraying or accusing over Venetians."

Jennifer shivered, though the room was not cold, and she felt the fine hair rise along her arms.

"This room also leads to the Bridge of Sighs. Shall we go on to see that, too?" Mario bent close to Jennifer. Unnecessarily close, she thought uncomfortably.

"Why, yes, let's see that, too," she said a little too quickly. Strange how she felt affected by the eerie atmosphere of this room of betrayal. It was all long ago, true, but the agony of those who fearfully waited here when they had been summoned seemed to pervade the air.

She felt a hand on her arm, and, startled, she whipped around to find Scott, his head bent, his voice low. "I'm certain that the man from last night has been following us, the one from the plane who was in Florian's."

Jennifer lifted her head to gaze around Scott's shoulder, letting her eyes search through the straggle of other sightseers who were roaming from room to room.

Turning back to Scott, she said, "I see absolutely no one who looks familiar, certainly no one who resembles our friend from last night."

In some exasperation, she remarked coolly, "Scott, if you did see the poor man, no doubt he's doing exactly what we're doing, seeing the famous places of Venice. After all, isn't the Doge's Palace a must on everyone's list? So . . . *please!*"

She looked away from him. This was rapidly growing worse and worse. He thought he was seeing things last night, and again this morning. Threat where none existed. He was almost as bad as her father or Uncle Henry, and no doubt these baseless "scares" were going to haunt her every move from now on until she could rid herself of him. Jennifer scowled darkly without realizing she was doing so.

Mario reached over to smooth out her brow with a gentle finger. "Temper, temper! Don't let these things bother you. After all, Scott is only trying to justify your uncle's trust. I'm all in favor of his being vigilant where your safety is concerned. What I object to is his never allowing us to be alone together. It's difficult to give romance its head when someone is standing by you with an interested smile."

Scott had fallen back to walk with Angelina, no doubt still on the lookout. Jennifer was almost sorry he hadn't caught Mario's protest, though he'd certainly heard versions of it before. Frankly, she'd rather have reversed the whole thing. With Mario's present amorous approach, she'd just as soon have Scott around to act as a possible retardant. But not have him so blasted vigilant about her own personal safety.

"Very well, everyone, on to the Bridge of Sighs and the famous or infamous prisons it leads to." Mario touched Jennifer's elbow, guiding her toward the bridge, the unhappy passageway to imprisonment. Jennifer fell silent as they approached it.

The covered bridge was gently arched, and, she decided, quite beautiful with its intricately grilled windows, had one not known its ugly history. The prisoners' last glimpse of freedom must have been from these windows, and the thought made her stop momentarily to gaze through them at the canal below.

As they approached the entrance to the prisons, a guide stepped forward then halted to bow respectfully to Mario. In a polite, deferential voice he murmured in Italian to Mario, who smiled, said something back, and then turned to his companions.

"By all rules and regulations, we are supposed to have a guide take us through the prisons, but Enzio here, and I, are long acquainted, and to be truthful, he knows that I am as familiar with the twists and turns of the prison as he is. As a child I used to go romping through them, scaring myself with old wives' tales of torture. So he is allowing me to be your guide today."

The guide grinned, apparently understanding what Mario was saying.

As they walked along the halls, the prisons didn't seem especially frightening, and Jennifer said so to Mario.

He put his hand over hers to tuck it in the crook of his elbow. "Ah, yes, my love, but wait until we get to the *pozzi*, the lower cellblocks, below the waterline, and from time to time flooded by high tides."

"And the prisoners?" she asked hesitantly, and immediately wished she hadn't.

"One can imagine," Mario said. "They drowned, of course, rather unpleasantly. Though don't look so disturbed, I do hear that some prisoners not only survived their imprisonment but actually flourished, though it's hard to imagine."

Jennifer's steps slowed as they approached the dank, dark dungeons, and they began walking single file, peering into the dismal holes. Mario, walking ahead, pulled out a small pencil flashlight to illuminate the deepening gloom as they penetrated farther into the *pozzi*.

How it happened, Jennifer could not be certain, but somehow she fell behind; perhaps it was when she halted momentarily to tighten the strap on one of her sandals. When she looked up, the light was gone and there was not the slightest sign of the dim shapes of her companions up ahead.

She stood still for a second, trying to decide whether to call or plunge right ahead until she caught up with them. At that moment, from in back of her, came the sound of footsteps. Jennifer turned slowly about. It couldn't be her friends, because they were on ahead. She could just barely make out the vague outline of a tall, thin form moving toward her.

Another tourist, of couse. Her mind tried nervously to reassure her: of course, it was nothing to worry about. Still, a gnawing little uncertainty made her whip about and hurry as fast as she could along the hall ahead. Once, she stopped a fraction of a second to listen, head cocked to one side, as she strained to hear. They were still coming on, those soft footsteps, a little faster now. Jennifer's mouth went dry, and her breath grew uneven.

Now she bolted headlong through the hall, coming up abruptly against a blank wall. Swerving almost without hesitation, she fled to the left, following the narrow aisle into even deeper darkness. She dared not call out, lest she point out her location to the follower. She couldn't be sure the others had even gone this way; they might not hear her, but the one pursuing her could.

In spite of her effort to resist, panic overcame her, and she began giving dry little panting sobs. Blinking back hot tears, she plunged blindly on. Now another corner to swerve frantically around, almost into the arms of someone holding a match above his head.

"Scott!" she gasped, grabbing at him frantically, holding to him tightly, head pressed against his chest, feeling the reassuring sound of his heart thumping. She couldn't speak, only whimpering little sobs coming from her in spite of all she could do to stop them.

"Jennifer, you little fool!" Scott spoke harshly. "You know better than to separate from us. Anything could happen. Where were you?" Then, apparently realizing something was radically wrong, he said urgently, "What is it, Jennifer? Come on, speak up, tell me!"

"I don't know what's wrong . . ." she mumbled unevenly against the roughness of his jacket. "It was . . . I thought someone was coming up behind me. I didn't know, so I ran."

The match had gone out, and Jennifer was relieved, for slowly she was beginning to feel silly and embarrassed. At least he couldn't see her face clearly. Why had she given way to panic? And why didn't she pull away from Scott now, instead of clutching him like a scared child?

There was a sudden sound ahead, and Jennifer felt herself thrust away and in back of Scott protectively as he lit a new match and strained to see ahead.

Out of the gloom came Mario's voice. "Find her yet, Scott?" He and Angelina moved forward toward them. "Ah, there you are, Jennifer, you gave us a scare for a few moments. You get lost?" Mario asked, the tiny flashlight playing on Jennifer's face, bringing a startled reaction from him.

"You've been crying! You're hurt!"

"N-n-no," stammered Jennifer. "Scared is all." Her heart still beat heavily in her throat, her ears. She felt confused. She hadn't been all that frightened, had she?

"Come on, let's get out of here." Mario took her arm. "We've seen quite enough of the prison."

"Look, you three go on ahead. I'll join you outside in a few minutes. I'm going to take a little look around," Scott said. "Keep a sharp eye on her, will you, Mario?"

"Of course! How about taking my flashlight? It's not very effective, but some of these passages are pretty shadowy. We won't need it. We'll be heading up to the next floor area right away, where it's light."

They turned to go, with Scott going back the way Jennifer had come. Mario called after him, "We'll wait for you in front of Florian's!"

"Okay!" Scott's voice came back to them as the small probing light moved around the corner.

With Mario holding to Jennifer's hand firmly, the three of them went slowly toward the stairway, the semi-darkness becoming full daylight.

In contrast, the sun was blindingly bright as they exited from the prisons and the Doge's Palace.

Angelina turned to look at Jennifer closely. "Are you certain you're all right? You look a little pale. Would you rather stop the sightseeing and go back to the *palazzo* as soon as Scott joins us?" Her soft voice sounded worried.

"No, really, I'm fine now," Jennifer replied more steadily. "I suppose I've been overconditioned by the way Scott's been imagining would-be kidnappers everywhere we go. It's bound to have an effect subconsciously, and when I saw someone in back of me . . . well, I just turned and ran . . . for no reason at all." She was a little surprised her words came out sounding fairly reasonable, for her thoughts were wheeling around in a weird kind of turmoil. And she wasn't sure why.

And so, led by Mario, they walked across St. Mark's Square to sit at one of the outside tables in front of Florian's.

The waiter, moving adeptly as a bullfighter, made his way through the crowded tables to halt at theirs. *"Buon giorno, eccelènza!"*

Mario acknowledged the greeting and ordered coffee.

As the man left, Jennifer looked at Mario questioningly. "May I ask why he said that?"

"*Buon giorno?* Good day." Then Mario shrugged and said, "That isn't what you meant, really, is it? One always hates to explain that. It sounds . . . rather archaic and strange to foreigners. It means, actually, 'excellency,' or, I suppose, more properly, 'your excellency,' but it is merely a polite term now, it means nothing more. It's a carry-over from the days when titles and positions meant a good deal more than they do now. It doesn't mean that I'm part of the royal family"—he smiled at her—"only that the family bears a title."

The Forlenzas, Jennifer decided, with the part of her mind that seemed to be still functioning halfway, were certainly a revered and well-known family in Venice.

For a little while the three of them watched the tourists and children feeding the pigeons that flocked about, the birds crowding each other, fluttering angry wings at any interloper trying to snatch a morsel away.

"Did you really see someone, someone that was . . . well, threatening?" Angelina raised long silky lashes as she eyed Jennifer over a tiny cup of *espresso*. "Or does it bother you to talk about it? You were really frightened, weren't you?"

Jennifer set her own cup down on the marble tabletop. "Yes, I suppose I was, for the moment. It was simply not being sure of who was coming up behind me. If . . . if there hadn't been all this silly furor ahead of time about a kidnapping, I'd never have noticed or cared someone was behind me. And, as I've said, Scott hasn't exactly minimized the kidnapping rumor."

Almost as if her mentioning him had conjured him up, Scott came striding across the wide square to join them. His face revealed nothing.

"See any signs of . . . of the fellow we saw last night, out here anywhere?" Scott asked.

The three facing him from across the table looked their embarrassed chagrin. "Sorry, old man, it simply didn't occur to us," Mario apologized. "Did you find anyone in there?"

Scott shook his head as he took his place at the table. "I really didn't expect I would, but there was always the chance."

Jennifer leaned toward him slightly. "Scott, please, let's just forget the whole subject for now. Let's just say that I panicked. I wouldn't have . . . but all this talk . . . the way you keep . . ."

He looked at her levelly, gray eyes suddenly darkening. "You were scared, scared as hell, don't tell me you weren't. Deep down inside, you know there's possible danger. You know why I'm along. I'll earn my pay."

"May a noncombatant get in on this?" Mario's voice interrupted them. "I realize this is between you two, but I want to stick in a question of my own that's at least partially related to what you're talking about."

Scott and Jennifer turned to look at him questioningly.

"Perhaps this is the time to decide if you two would like to call off the sightseeing?" Mario asked calmly. "We could return to the *palazzo*, as Angelina suggested. No doubt it would be safer to do so if Jennifer's fright may have some basis for concern. Or . . . of course, we can continue . . . ?" He lifted a shoulder quizzically.

"Well . . ." began Scott reluctantly, but Jennifer, sensing he was going to say to go back, cut across his words briskly.

"Return? No!" she said fervently. "When we finish our coffee, let's go on with our original plan." She did not look at Scott.

"Okay with you, Mitchell?" Mario asked confirmation.

"Ummm, I suppose so," Scott said without much enthusiasm. "But stick close in the future, Jennifer, where we can keep an eye on you."

The retort she would have liked to make, she swallowed. Four more weeks, she groaned inwardly, carefully masking her expression so no one would read her thoughts. But, no, she corrected herself, not four—just one more. Then he'd be standing openmouthed and startled . . . and alone.

"You're smiling now. Nice thoughts, maybe?" Mario asked teasingly.

"Oh, very nice indeed. You've no idea," Jennifer said, then realized a little belatedly she needn't have sounded quite so spirited in her reply, for it brought a sudden suspicious look from Scott.

They walked, they climbed stairs, moved through the museums, strolled up over the small humpbacked bridges, down through alleys that curved and wound tortuously in and around shops and houses. And they were not alone; tourists and local residents were so numerous that it seemed all Venice was in constant migration.

The memory of the prisons faded to almost nothing but a small faint cloud crouched at the edge of Jennifer's mind. The only way it made itself known at all was by a slightly flustered feeling that refused to go away.

Late in the day, as the sun was going down, splattering the waters of the canal with a bronze luster, they returned to their gondola.

"I'm tired," Jennifer said happily, glad to sink down in the cushioned seat. "The nice kind of tired that's made up of all the lovely things we did and saw." Turning, she smiled at Mario. "And that lunch! Is every place as good as that . . . that . . . Graspo . . . Graspo . . . " She stumbled over the name.

"Graspo de Ua." Mario leaned toward her, lifting her chin with his hand, looking deep into her blue eyes, speaking almost absently.

Jennifer wanted to twist her head away, but could think of no gracious way to do so, so she tried another diverting tactic. "Mario, it's still broad daylight, people are passing in other boats . . . This looks . . . a little intimate!" She gave him a wobbling smile in an effort to sound light, airy, and not at all rude.

It worked. He sat back unperturbed. "Very well, dear Jennifer, you are reprieved for the moment!" He scowled fiercely, eyes dancing, belying the scowl. "But, beware, you shall pay for the respite when we're alone. If . . . if we ever are!" He shot a quick reproachful look at Scott's broad shoulders.

Angelina twisted around in her seat to call back to them. "Jennifer, look ahead, this may be new to you."

Slashing through the water, red light flashing, siren shrilling, came a motorboat. As it passed them, rocking the light gondola with a rolling wake, Jennifer could see it was an ambulance.

"Everything by water," she gasped, "even an ambulance!"

"And if it reaches its destination too late, or if the person dies later, he makes his last watery crossing by boat, too," Mario said. "Usually by gondola, for he is no longer in a hurry, especially to the cemetery on San Michele Island."

As they stepped out of the gondola after it had drawn up at the *palazzo,* they went inside, to find a worried-looking countess hurrying out of the salon where they'd had *aperitivi* the evening before.

"My dear Jennifer," she said rapidly, her gentle face drawn with concern, "for you, many times, the *telefono!* From America. It is . . . it is . . ." She halted, apparently her command of English vanishing momentarily in her anxiety, causing her to turn to Mario and speak quickly in Italian.

He relayed the message to Jennifer. "You are to call the telephone operator at once. A matter of some importance, I gather."

Something had happened to her father! Jennifer's face whitened at the thought. "The phone," she requested anxiously, "I'll call right away!"

Angelina and Scott stepped aside to stand by the countess as Mario led Jennifer into a nearby room where she could phone. He dialed the operator, and with his help the call went through. Turning, he handed the phone to Jennifer, then tactfully stepped outside into the hall.

"Hello, hello!" Jennifer spoke tensely, voice thin and strained. There was a crackle of sound along the line; then, as the person at the other end began talking, she listened, her mouth tightening. Her face, which had been pale, began gradually to redden.

"I'm all right, Uncle Henry, I'm perfectly all right! I have no doubt I shall stay that way! We were out sightseeing, yes, all day. But, Uncle Henry . . . Uncle Henry . . ."

she had to wait while he protested at her outing when he
had tried to get through to her. "But, Uncle Henry, I
came to Italy to see the sights, not stay inside. I tell you,
it's perfectly safe. Why you and Father ever took seriously
the rumor . . ."

She halted at the torrent of words from her uncle,
slashing into her conversation, riding over her thoughts,
exactly the way he always had.

"But, Uncle Henry, I . . ." she tried again, but failed.
What she was getting over transatlantic telephone was
nothing but a replay, word for word, of a lecture she
knew by heart. Yes, she finally agreed, she would be careful, yes, she'd leave word where she could be reached
when she left Venice. She drummed irritably with her
fingers on the table beside her.

The instructions, laced with warnings, went on . . . and
on, punctuated only by her occasional weary "Yes, Uncle Henry." It was, she reminded herself, a weak way to
handle the matter; she should have stood up to him, but
unless one knew Uncle Henry and his reputation as a
successful, nationally famous lawyer who achieved that
fame by his bombastic relentless style . . . well, if someone
didn't know how Uncle Henry operated, there was no use
in trying to explain why it was easier just to say
"Yes, Uncle Henry."

At last he concluded by saying, "All right, just see
that you do! And put Mitchell on the line. He's there,
isn't he?" Not a single question in his voice. If Henry
Leland Hudson told his employee to stick close to her,
the employee would do just that.

Jennifer set the phone down, pivoted, and walked into
the hall, lips firm, shoulders rigid. Mario, his mother,
Angelina, and Scott were still there, waiting, their faces
turning anxiously toward her as she approached.

"Something wrong at home?"

Jennifer shook her head, trying to control her resentment at Uncle Henry's diatribe. "No," she said tightly,
"it's my Uncle Henry. He wants to speak to you, Scott."

Inside, she was fuming. To think that her uncle would
take it upon himself to usurp her father's role this way,

lecturing her, laying down rules of what she could do or couldn't do! But why should she be surprised? she reminded herself reproachfully. This was the way he'd always acted, as if she were a six-year-old child, a backward one at that.

Scott, after a quick look at her flushed face, had gone in to the phone.

Jennifer spoke ruefully to the others. "Sorry to sound so irritable, but my uncle . . ." She shrugged helplessly. "I do realize his concern is well-meant, but it's so . . . so overpowering. He does go on and on."

Mario cocked his head inquiringly. "Still worrying about the kidnapping rumor, is he?"

Jennifer nodded. "Yes, and now I suppose he's reinforcing his orders to Scott. I hope Scott doesn't say anything about today at the prison."

"Still," Angelina said thoughtfully, "I suppose there's been news of the numerous kidnappings in Italy recently. No doubt he's read of them, and that disturbs him even more."

Jennifer, her anger ebbing away, smiled. "I'm certain he's read every word."

The countess touched Jennifer's arm with a gentle pale hand. "But, it is to be careful, the world is not so safe these days. We wish nothing to happen to you, my dear."

Jennifer thanked her, then, saying she thought she'd go up to her room to change clothes, perhaps rest a few moments before dinner, took her leave, giving a quick, curious glance at the room where Scott was apparently still on the phone to her uncle, as she went on upstairs.

As she closed the door to her room behind her, Jennifer kicked off her shoes and padded across the floor, unzipping her dress as she went, heading for the shower.

6

———

Refreshed after bathing, Jennifer stood before the mirror, briskly toweling her auburn hair, her mind busy with a jumble of thoughts, each one struggling for recognition. There was no use thinking about Uncle Henry; nothing was ever going to change him. And what did he say to Scott?

Scott. Her hands were suddenly still. For some reason, one she couldn't account for, she didn't want to think about him; her mind swerved away, as one quickly snatches a hand back from a hot stove. But, stubbornly, she forced herself not to be so silly. Why, she demanded of herself, was she reacting this way?

Frowning, she gazed unseeingly into the mirror. Then, abruptly, her brow cleared and she shrugged in relief. That was it, that was it exactly! It was simple, really. Of course, it was because Scott was Uncle Henry's henchman, and through Scott her uncle was still trying to manage her affairs.

As she dressed, it was mainly Mario who began occupying her thoughts. Right now it seemed as if one week would be quite long enough to remain here in Venice. She liked Mario, but the key word was still "like," which wasn't quite enough. Angelina was delightful with her bright warm friendliness, Mario's mother was gentle and charming, they were all very kind. Jennifer paused as she bent to slip on her shoes. She really wished she could fall in love with Mario.

The shrill whistle of a *vaporetto* passing by on the canal below drew her irresistibly to the balcony, to once again stand watching the ever-changing panorama the enigmatic city.

"Jennifer." Scott's voice startled her.

She turned to see him coming out onto the balcony from his room. "Get your orders of the day from good old Uncle Henry?" she asked wryly.

He nodded absently, his mind clearly on something else. Running his hand through his hair, clearing his throat, he gave her an apprehensive look.

"This seems the only place we can have a private conversation," he said. His hands were thrust deep in his pockets.

"Yes?" Jennifer replied, wondering what was coming.

She didn't have long to wait. He began cautiously. "I'm going to have to get a little personal, if you don't mind."

She quirked an eyebrow at him. "I do mind, of course. That kind of statement always means there is something unpleasant to follow."

Exasperation and impatience appeared to vie for control in his face, and for a moment she thought he was going to whip around and stalk right back into his room. Instead, he took a sharp breath and said, "I'm here to watch out for you, as unpleasant as you clearly find it." He hesitated, frowned, brushed his hand through his hair again, and said, "I don't like this any better than you will, but, my friend, here goes: Has it occurred to you that maybe the Forlenzas are pretty short of money? Had a good look at the place? All run down, needs repair, plenty of it, staffed by a pair of ancient servants who probably aren't getting much in the way of salary. And what does friend Mario do for a living? He seems to have an awful lot of free time."

"I don't know what he does," Jennifer answered coolly. And it really needn't be any of her business, she could have added, but decided not to.

"You met in the States, right? Well, what was he doing there? Working or just visiting?"

"Working *and* visiting. He was some kind of adviser on

a film that someone was making about Italy. And, may I ask, just what business is it of yours?"

"Plenty. Your uncle filled me in on a lot—"

"I'll just bet he did!" Jennifer snapped bitterly. "He probably had a detective hired as well as a bodyguard!" Suddenly her eyes flashed blue fire. "Don't tell me— that's what he had on his mind today! He didn't actually hire . . ." Fury halted her voice, but she glared at Scott.

Scott's face reddened right up to his hairline. "Okay, so maybe he did. Maybe with good reason. Anyhow, it all goes back to the fact that Mario is on the shorts. Off and on, he's had a government job, prestige kind of thing. The family name carries some weight still. But the old monarchy party doesn't have power or . . . votes, these days, so he's odd man out. And, like a lot of others, over-qualified for the jobs around. So . . . to put it bluntly, he needs money. To run this place, for one thing."

"And . . . ?" she said frostily.

"And what way would there be to get a lot of money, tax-free, in a hurry . . . than by a kidnapping?"

Jennifer looked at him incredulously. "Just a minute. Do I understand just what you're hinting? Do you actually mean to say you think Mario . . . that he . . . ?" She had to stop and take a deep steadying breath before she could continue.

"Scott Mitchell, you make me sick! You really do! That is the most ridiculous thing I've ever heard! For one thing, Mario isn't the type of person who'd ever even consider—"

"Yes?" Scott cut in acidly. "How would you know? How many potential kidnappers do you number among your acquaintances? Or are you some kind of amateur living-room psychiatrist? This job wouldn't have so many drawbacks if I didn't have to constantly cope with a stubborn, completely naive . . ." He stopped, clearly searching for a further unflattering description of her.

"Thank you," Jennifer's voice was icy cold with barely restrained ire. "We've done that little act several times before, and, I might say, it isn't any more interesting this time around. However, you're right, I don't know any kidnappers socially, though perhaps you do. Besides, it may have escaped your notice that Mario . . . why Mario . . ."

He lifted a cynical eyebrow at her. "Oh, you're sure?"

"It's barely possible that Mario has a different interest in me, other than the hope of kidnapping. I happen to know. His intentions, to quote a Victorian phrase, are strictly honorable," she said loftily.

"Perhaps. Or perhaps that's what you're supposed to think. Doesn't it seem at all interesting to you that your invitation to visit coincided, more or less, with the kidnap rumor?"

She turned around to gaze out at the scenery, saying calmly, "I was planning to come to Europe anyway. When Mario heard that, he invited me to spend some time with them, him and his family, in Venice. And, Scott Mitchell," she said impatiently, "you are beginning to sound exactly like Uncle Henry. And act like him! Tend to your own business and leave me to mine!"

Jennifer whipped around and brushed past him, starting to go to her room, her enjoyment of the scenery now completely spoiled. But Scott shot out a hand to grasp her wrist firmly, halting her.

"Just a moment, Jennifer, I'm serious. I can't ignore some pretty fishy coincidences. If you want to, all right, but I'm going to conduct myself in a way that I feel is right and judicious. *And* cautious. One thing more. You will please not say anything about my suspicions to Mario."

That wasn't a request, it was an out-and-out order. Jennifer yanked her wrist sharply from his grasp and darted into her room, locking the French windows behind her. Sinking down on a green satin-slipper chair, breathing unsteadily, she seethed inside.

The nerve of him, telling her what she could do and what she couldn't do! Just because he worked for Uncle Henry didn't mean he had to copy him. Jennifer was glad she'd told him so.

Glancing down at her wrist, she was mildly surprised to find there was no mark upon it where he'd grasped her, for she could still feel the touch of those firm fingers against her skin. She stared at the wrist for a full minute, then glanced up at the French windows leading to the balcony, a puzzled, uncertain look in her eyes.

Then she gazed about the room, the faded fresco on the wall vividly reminding her of Scott's words. The *palazzo* was indeed in need of repair . . . the servants . . . the missing Canaletto that Mario had mentioned—he'd said there once had been two.

Somehow the memory of stories she'd read about the shabby gentility of the Deep South after the Civil War floated through her mind, the tales of the valiant effort to keep up the old ways in spite of poverty, of old servants who had been slaves, but stayed on because they, too, had no place else to go.

But kidnapping . . . No! She shoved the thought away harshly. That she would never believe in connection with Mario. Still, there was something else that Scott's questions and comments had stirred up, perhaps something that had been there all the time since she had arrived. That was the matter of why Mario had become so unexpectedly vigorous in his amorous pursuit of her. Was it, then, her father's money that had caused it? If that was really the source of his interest in her, it was unflattering, to say the least.

Jennifer glanced down at her watch. Soon it would be time to descend the stairs and be with Mario again . . . with that nagging little speculation as difficult to ignore as a tiny sharp pebble in a shoe. That disturbing thought thrust her out of her chair and spurred her to walking restlessly about the room.

Damn Scott Mitchell anyhow, she thought irritably. Why had he brought the subject up? Oh, sure, his angle was all concentrated on the kidnapping possibility, which was absurd, but he had underlined the need for money by the Forlenzas, and that, unhappily, supplied a reason for Mario's change in attitude toward her.

And now, with this in the back of her mind, she was going to have to be with Mario this evening, not acting any different, not showing signs of that nasty little thorn pricking at her thoughts. It wasn't, she reflected, as if you could clear the air by asking straight out, "Say, Mario, is the reason for your increased interest in me because of the money my father has . . . that will be mine someday?" She made a rueful face. It didn't matter anyhow; she wasn't planning to marry him.

But a little later, when she joined Mario, she felt reassured. He was so cheerful, so charming, so outrageously affectionate in an almost amusing way, she found it impossible to even consider the idea he might be a possible kidnapper, nor even, really, a fortune hunter.

Scott, too, despite his heated statements earlier, presented an untroubled face and manner, with only a quick warning flick in his eyes when they met hers in passing.

After dinner, some friends of Mario's and Angelina's dropped by to meet the young woman from America. They looked quizzically at Scott, clearly wondering why a guest of Mario's should be accompanied by a young and certainly not unattractive man.

But Mario adroitly skirted the subject by explaining that Scott was another visitor, one who worked for Jennifer's uncle and happened to be arriving on the same plane. And he left it at that.

Jennifer's vague uneasiness eventually vanished under the gay and amusing conversations with the young Italians. They didn't all speak English, but they tried. Scott had said he knew very little Italian, yet he appeared to be perfectly at ease in the Latin tongue. But the visitors turned eagerly upon Jennifer, watching her with their liquid dark eyes, stumbling and laughing through their halting English. Then they insisted on teaching her words and fragments of sentences of Italian, cheering on her efforts with such gaiety and exuberance that the evening flew by, causing Jennifer, when she looked at her watch, to look again in amazement.

And they had plans to go to the Lido tomorrow morning, she and Mario, Angelina and Scott. Hopefully, not early!

When she went up to bed, Scott, as usual, was right

behind her. And, as usual, tried to halt her at the door for a few words in private.

"Jennifer," he began, and she had the immediate feeling it was something more about Mario, something she simply didn't want to hear.

So she yawned, lifting her fingers to cover her mouth daintily, then sighed. "Please, if you don't mind, Scott, not tonight. I'm very tired. Another time."

With that she escaped through her door, shutting it quickly behind her. Then she grinned. That had been a bit naughty of her, leaving him standing there, that frustrated look on his face! But she really wasn't interested in hearing more about Mario's being a threat to her safety. She knew he wasn't. And the money thing didn't matter either, even if it were true. But she couldn't believe that, either.

When she tumbled into bed, she gave a last glance at her traveling clock by the bedside. It was nearly two-thirty. She groaned. "Please, nobody wake me up early!"

And it wasn't early. In fact, by the time their boat had crossed the Venetian lagoon to the sandy white beach of the Lido next morning, it was nearly lunchtime. Leaving the dock, they strolled down the boulevard that curved between two lines of trees, the beach itself lined with hundreds of cabins and dressing rooms, the brilliant blue of the water just beyond.

"Bathe or lunch first?" Mario smiled down at Jennifer.

She laughed. "With breakfast barely finished? I choose bathing . . . if it's all right with the rest of you?" Turning, she asked Angelina.

The Italian girl nodded. "I'm with you, Jennifer. At this moment, I couldn't face another meal. Let's find a cabana and change. Two cabanas at the very least, gentlemen!" she ordered.

After slipping into their bathing suits, the two girls made their way across the sand to join Scott and Mario at the place designated to meet, circling around bronzing bodies, oiled and languid, stretched out under the sun.

"Your American movie stars like our Lido," Angelina said, nodding toward a famous film couple who were strolling down the beach toward the water. "Everyone who is anyone in the world of wealth or fashion . . . or just in the gossip columns, turns up here sooner or later," she added.

Mario was standing, watching for them, his slim well-proportioned body and olive skin a target for feminine eyes nearby, Jennifer noticed. There was no doubt about it, Mario was an extraordinarily handsome man, certainly charismatic, and she, Jennifer, was an absolute fool not to fall in love with him. And another fool was Scott, for even considering Mario a potential kidnapper.

Mario's eyes deepened with approval as he gazed at Jennifer. "You are lovely, *cara*. All the men are jealous of me!"

Jennifer laughed at him. "Mario, you're impossible! It's your sister they're staring at."

And well they might, Jennifer realized. Angelina's wisp of bathing suit only accented the reason she was a model. The golden skin, the graceful lines of her figure, the black shining hair, loosened now, cascaded about her slim shoulders. The Forlenzas were a formidable pair, Jennifer thought, and as charming and unassuming as they were good-looking.

"Where's my nemesis?" Jennifer cast a quick look about.

"He said he was going to take a quick dip in the water before you got here. I think he wants to be back when you arrive from changing, to get back on the job!" Mario grinned.

Apparently Mario was right, for Scott came walking toward them now, slicking water off his arms with the flat of his hands. Drops still beaded on his bronzed shoulders, and Jennifer noticed Mario wasn't the only one who was catching feminine attention. Dandy! Let them, she thought irritably. They didn't know him! What was that he'd called her last night—naive . . . stubborn? Reluctantly she had to admit he could be right about the "stubborn." But she certainly wasn't naive. And *he*—he was an unmitigated bother!

They bathed in the cool water, they sunned, they

strolled up to one of the sidewalk cafés for lunch. Jennifer was intrigued by the sight of so many familiar faces among those strolling by, familiar for having been seen in movies or television or on the front pages in connection with the latest scandal. Angelina was right, Jennifer thought; they all seemed to be here.

She said so. "In a way, it's almost like watching the night of the Academy Awards, Angelina."

The other girl was lifting a spoonful of *vichyssoise* and looking at it lovingly. "Calories, delicious calories! I shall suffer a month of self-denial for having succumbed. The bitter life of a model! But you're correct about the people here. Sooner or later everyone turns up."

That prediction was proved correct almost immediately.

"Jennie! Welcome to the Lido! What took you so long to get here?" Craig Holman, blond hair looking even more bleached by the sun, stood beside the table; a lovely porcelain-cheeked young woman wearing a wide blue sun hat was standing beside him.

There was a flurry of introductions. Jennifer was conscious that Craig was eyeing her companions with those alert curious eyes of his. The young woman with him was charming, soft-spoken, very much a lady, and quite different from Craig's usual swinging, bright-haired, ample-bosomed girls. She was really quite beautiful, Jennifer decided, her classic features delightfully challenged by a faint powdering of freckles across her nose.

But Mario was stepping forward, taking the girl's hand in his. "Constance, Constance Hunter! I didn't recognize you at first. You've grown up!"

He turned to the others. "Excuse me, please, but I used to know Constance when she was a little girl in a ponytail, with freckles." He peered at her affectionately. "Which I observe you still have! Her brother and I were in school in England together, and I used to visit at his home in Kent on holidays. And Constance . . ."

She wrinkled her nose at him ruefully. "I was fourteen to your twenty, and I had braces on my teeth. You were so insufferably adult!" She laughed.

"I've heard Mario speak of you and your brother, Derek, your whole family," Angelina said warmly. "You were very kind to him, all of you."

Invited to join the group, the two newcomers sat around the table. The conversation was quick and sparkling. Jennifer was aware, however, of Craig's faintly discernible dismay that Mario's earlier acquaintance with Constance was diverting her attention away from himself. He shifted uncomfortably in his chair, and when he met Jennifer's eyes, gave a wincing little shrug that he covered up so quickly she felt no one else had noticed.

Mario turned to Craig. "Will you and Constance have dinner with us this evening? Please do. I ask you not to rob me of the opportunity to repay, if only in small part, the hospitality the Hunter family offered me in England seven years ago."

To Jennifer's surprise, Craig appeared pleased to accept, after a quick questioning look at Constance. That was a little strange. She'd have thought he'd have preferred to be alone with the English girl, especially under the circumstances. However, he more than likely felt it was a difficult-to-refuse invitation.

Scott, seemingly relaxed, joined in the lighthearted conversation being batted back and forth about the table, but it did seem to Jennifer that he was, at the same time, carefully appraising the newcomers, running them under his suspicious eye. Next, she supposed, there'd be another period of quizzing her about Craig, once he got her alone. And there was Constance. Surely he wouldn't extend his distrust to include her. Still, Jennifer wouldn't put it past Scott to do just that—he had such a one-track mind.

Though Mario teased Constance, reminding her how very scruffy and disheveled she often looked as an adolescent, it was obvious that he, as the others, was fully appreciative of her cool beauty now.

For the rest of the day the six of them strolled about together, watching people play tennis at one of the courts, or else they walked down to the water's edge, leaving six sets of footprints in the wet sand. It was a pleasant time, marred only by Scott's constant vigil, the quick way he craned his head to watch anyone who seemed to linger in the vicinity too long, or what he thought was too long.

But it marred it only for Jennifer, for the rest of the group seemed unaware of his constant air of suspicion. Once or twice Jennifer gave Scott a warning shake of her head and a faint scowl, trying as best she could to dissuade him from continuing, but he only slanted back a stubborn stare before turning his head to chat with one of the others.

After they had changed clothes and started back in the direction of the dock to take their departure from the Lido, Craig moved up close to Jennifer to talk to her alone, his voice curious. "What's this Scott guy all about? Funny, I got the idea on the plane that he was merely someone who happened to work in your uncle's law office and that he was on the same flight by sheer circumstance. Now he turns up here with you. Isn't that a little hard on your current romance?"

It was the gossiper who peered out from his eyes. But she couldn't merely shrug and say it was all coincidence, all of it, so she tried for a casual few words of truth.

"Well, Craig, you know my father and how overprotective he is?"

He nodded his blond head. "It's not a well-kept secret among your friends."

"Same old story. He's afraid of a kidnap—that's the reason for Scott." There, the bare bones of truth.

He looked at her blankly for a moment; then there was a twitch of his mouth, followed by his whole face cracking up with hilarity. "Jennie, baby, you don't mean it! Your old man actually sends you off to Europe with a handsome young dude for your *protection*? Don't tell me, I can't stand it!" He roared with laughter. "My God, Jennie, it's like turning a fox loose to protect a little baby chick! Tell me, does he also have orders to sleep in your bedroom, to keep a watchful eye on you?"

There was an uncomfortable reminder in that comment, and Jennifer snapped angrily, "Don't be crude, Craig Holman!" Then she looked at him suspiciously. "And don't you dare go babbling that wherever you go!"

He was wiping his eyes as he grinned at her. "Oh, now, Jennie, don't ask that. It's the funniest damned thing I've heard this year. Hasn't anyone ever told your old man about the birds and the bees?"

The others had turned in surprise to look at Craig. "What's wrong . . . or right?" Mario asked curiously. "Share it with us?"

"It's nothing," Jennifer put in quickly, in an effort to prevent Craig's repeating his own version of Scott's job for the entertainment of the group.

She was rescued by the boat's arrival at that fortunate moment, and the matter was lost in the farewells and promises for a reunion a little later for dinner at the *palazzo*.

On their way back down the Grand Canal, Mario was as attentive as ever, with that same little hint of possessiveness in his voice. Jennifer smiled and fended him off as deftly and gracefully as she could, but his attitude revived that uneasy feeling in her mind. Again she wondered uncomfortably if there wasn't something too carefully calculated, too deliberate in his pursuit of her. She gave a mental shake of her head, as if to scold herself for being, in her own way, as suspicious of people's intentions as Scott. What she should be doing was enjoying Mario's company, politely discouraging him, and not taking the whole thing as a serious matter.

That evening, when she dressed for dinner, she chose from her closet a long white chiffon dinner dress, as soft and flowing as a trail of sea foam. As she slipped into it, she was aware of how well it became her, snug bodice, slim at the waist, the full skirt cascading to the floor.

The mirror reflected the smooth tan of her shoulders, the shining auburn of her hair. As she looked at herself speculatively for a long moment, she felt a faint flood of color under the smooth skin of her cheeks. Now, just for whom was she dressing so carefully? Mario? But wasn't she being a little hypocritical in wearing her most becoming dress if she meant to discourage him?

Craig, then? She gave a sharp, exasperated sigh. *Craig!* She was certain he was already elaborating on the story he was going to relate with amusement to all his continental pals. Certainly not Craig!

That left . . . well, it left only . . . Scott. She stared stonily at her reflection in the mirror. *Oh, yes, certainly Scott! You bet!* Jennifer compressed her lips. He was certainly the very *last* person in the world she'd make any effort for, that she'd want to impress. But she was startled by her heart's sudden uncontrollable jump. Jennifer turned away from the mirror hurriedly. Ridiculous! She brushed the disturbing little stirring of thought from her mind as one does unhappy or unpleasant subjects.

Going over to the French windows, she ever so gently twisted the latch, little by little, soundlessly, then opened the windows to peer out. He was not there, so she stepped quietly to the railing to spend a few solitary moments of enjoyment watching the Venetian panorama, needing to be alone, to blot everything else from her mind.

Pale wavering shadows of approaching night were slowly stealing across the dull silver of the water. Below her the small boats shuttled up and down the canal, a gondola passed with a pair of lovers, uncaring of witnesses, exchanging kisses.

How long she stood there, enchanted by the ever-changing pageant of Venice, she did not know, nor when he appeared behind her on the balcony.

But, as someone is uncannily aware of another's presence, she turned, to see Scott, standing in his doorway, watching her silently. As she looked at him, an unconscious frown already beginning to creep across her face, he lifted amused eyebrows.

"Well, I must say I'm impressed!" He nodded in approval as he let his eyes travel swiftly over the dress. "What is this to be, the final romantic coup de grace for poor old Mario? From what I've been observing, I shouldn't think any further effort on your part would be necessary."

"It's nothing of the sort!" Jennifer said frostily. "But it's the kind of comment I've come to expect from you. Besides, I thought you had the idea his interest in me was monetary and criminal. As for why I'm wearing this, both Angelina and Constance will be dressed the same way, in dinner dresses. And I don't know why I'm even bothering to make any explanation to you." She turned back to the railing deliberately.

He moved up to stand beside her, undaunted by her chilly response. "Well, let me give you a little advice, even if you don't want it. I'd just say you better be a little cautious in stirring up a hot-blooded male, even unintentionally. Remember, a Venetian . . . no, make that Mario, might be seized by 'an insatiate thirst of enjoying a greedily desired object.'" There was teasing in his voice. "Montaigne said that; it's not original with me."

She whirled to face him. "Scott Mitchell, I don't particularly enjoy your dabbling in my personal affairs. The way I understand it, you were sent along with me to do one thing. Act as a bodyguard. Not a *duenna*, not as a father-adviser. Just a bodyguard!" She said it so tartly that she was a little sorry. She hadn't meant to lose her temper, but he was so . . . so . . . presumptuous!

Scott leaned against the balcony railing, arms folded across his chest, eyeing her silently for a few seconds. Then, when he spoke, his voice was carefully expressionless.

"Very well, then, I'll speak in my official capacity. Let's have a little more detailed information about this Craig Holman. Not just that you've known him before. Where, who introduced you, exactly how long have you known him? And who is he?" He eyed her levelly. "Be specific."

Just as she thought he would be—back to Craig Holman with his eternal suspicions. "I'll answer your last question first. He's well known almost everywhere society people gather—spas, ski resorts, and the Lido, as we found today." Jennifer shrugged. "Just anywhere and everywhere he thinks might be fun or entertaining. I met him at Aspen; he's a cousin of a friend of mine. It was" —she paused, trying to remember—"two years, maybe three years ago. Why?" she asked bluntly.

He flicked Jennifer a knowing look. "Think about it. Guy is on the plane, turns up here in Venice. Coincidence?

Maybe. But only maybe. As your bodyguard"—he shot her a flat look—"I can't afford to take anyone or anything at face value. What's he do for a living?"

"I really don't know. I suppose he inherited money. If you plan to ask about Constance as the next on your list of suspects, I'm afraid you'll have to get that information from Mario or Craig." Then she had a sudden errant thought. "Just exactly what would you do if someone actually did attempt to kidnap me?" she asked abruptly.

His mouth creased in a stubborn line. "That's what I am trying to prevent—an attempt. I don't want it to get that far. Maybe it explains why I'm watching all the time, questioning, trying to avoid leaving an opening for someone to try to grab you."

"But if it should get that far, what would you do then?" she persisted curiously.

"I'd plan to stop it," Scott said shortly.

"How?" Jennifer really did want to know.

"Never mind how. That's my department." His eyes suddenly shuttered.

"Do you carry a gun? Is that how?" Jennifer's soft white dress stirred slightly as a breeze sprung up, sweeping gently across the balcony.

Scott looked back at her stolidly. "I said that's my department."

"I should think you'd have to have a license and that sort of thing, wouldn't you?" Jennifer waited for him to reply, and when he didn't, she gazed thoughtfully at his expressionless face. Now that she'd started this line of thought, she wanted to know to what lengths he felt her uncle expected him to go if necessary. Frankly, the thought of possible gunplay made her uneasy.

"But, Scott, if you . . . if you . . ." Abruptly she said, "I bet I know. You couldn't carry a weapon on an airline —there's a screening. And you couldn't bring one into another country through customs, unless . . . unless . . ." Her eyes narrowed suspiciously. "Uncle Henry at work again! I'll bet he got on the phone, called up one of his good old government cronies, and whispered national defense. He could make it sound that way if he wanted."

Scott shifted his position a trifle against the railing and at the same time allowed his gaze to wander casually away. But she noticed the faint show of color where his coat collar met his skin, the tightness of the muscles in his cheek.

"I can see I'm right in my guess," she said bitterly. "Why didn't he order a navy convoy, the air national guard, or a brigade of marines while he was about it?" She was absolutely exasperated and knew she looked it.

Now he turned back to face her, temper showing in his eyes. "Sometimes you drive me up the wall, Jennifer Cartwright! I don't like this job, please get that straight in your busy little mind, *I . . . don't . . . like . . . this . . . job.* You don't think the threat is real? Well, I'm not certain I do, either, and if the would-be kidnappers knew you as well as I'm getting to, they wouldn't be tempted for one damned minute. You're . . . headstrong! You may be attractive, but you're a royal pain in the neck!"

He was furious, she thought, he really was! Jennifer watched as he wheeled around and stalked angrily into his room, leaving her with a memory of his last glare.

The worst of it was, she reflected, that it struck her for the moment as incredibly funny. She had been irritated at Uncle Henry, true, but when she thought of that aloof, obstinate man, Scott, and how he had completely lost his temper just because she had uncovered his little secret—his and Uncle Henry's, and probably half of the United States Senate's or New York Police Department's, maybe even the CIA's—she couldn't help giggling. He was so furious. But Uncle Henry still left a sore spot, the way he had no inhibitions when it came to getting his wishes taken care of, and his own way about everything.

Turning, she walked back into her room, leaned toward the mirror to give her lips a final bit of color, then opened the door to go downstairs.

A stiff-backed Scott stood just outside in the hall,

waiting. "I apologize for what I said a minute ago," he murmured. "As was fairly obvious, I blazed out at you because I out and out lost my temper. Sorry about that, it won't happen again. Quite unfair of me." He spoke almost formally, looking uncomfortable.

She reached out to touch his arm lightly. "I'm sorry, too, Scott. It was mostly my doing. I let my curiosity get away from me. But"—suddenly she couldn't repress a smile—"it really was funny!"

For a second Scott looked disconcerted; then the stiffness went out of his shoulders, he relaxed, his grin appearing. "God, we're a pair, aren't we? Well, come on, let's go on down. But I warn you"—he suddenly turned serious once again—"I'm still on the job, and like it or not, you'll be getting the same supervision from me."

"I suppose so. But don't suspect my friends, if you don't mind. They're not international desperadoes in search of national secrets," she said over her shoulder as she started toward the stairs.

The evening was pleasant and amusing, Jennifer found; even Craig seemed genuinely relaxed, not even minutely resentful, at least as far as she could see, of the comfortable relationship between Constance and the handsome young count.

Jennifer glanced over at Mario, who was chatting animatedly with the English girl. His dark head was bent toward her silver-blond beauty, and there was no doubt that they were an extremely striking pair. What was quite obvious was the radiant air of affection between them. Jennifer was a little surprised that she felt no twinge of any kind, not jealousy, certainly. Which only demonstrated to her that her feeling for Mario was only platonic . . . and could never be anything more. But Craig . . . why didn't he object? Other than that first flurry of chagrin she had noted, he seemed to accept the situation.

In fact, Craig seemed quite interested in Angelina. They knew some of the same people in Paris, and he was regaling her with some of his wicked, amusing anecdotes. Did Scott mind, since he had appeared to be attracted to the stunning Latin beauty? Jennifer couldn't tell; he was sitting back in his chair, face inscrutable, offering an occasional casual comment.

Shortly after dinner, the countess had excused herself to go to her room, after again expressing her gratitude to Constance for her family's hospitality to Mario. It was later, much later that Craig and Constance took their leave, promising they'd all get together again the next day.

Jennifer was about to leave the salon to go up to her room, when Mario, speaking quietly, touched a delaying hand to her arm.

"Jennifer, let's evade your cortege of one. I like Scott, he's a nice chap, but don't you think it's a bit much to have him looking over our shoulders all the time? How about a few moments of our own, just the two of us? I'll summon the gondola, and we shall have a ride down the canal in the moonlight. It's a full moon tonight. Please, you mustn't miss it. The canal on a night like this is something poets could write about. And do."

"I . . . I . . ." Jennifer searched quickly for an excuse.

"Don't say no before I tell you that there is a *festa* tonight in one of the *campi*, and there will be many brilliant carnival lights reflecting on the waters of the canal."

At her inquiring look, he explained, "Sorry, *festa* is our word for what I've heard you Americans call 'fiesta.' *Campo* is 'town square.' At least, that's what we call it in Venice. It is only St. Mark's that is called truly a 'square' here. Please, Jennifer, I promise you, it will be an experience to remember."

"But, Mario, I . . . you . . ." she began uncertainly, conscious of Scott standing across the room, hands thrust in the pockets of his jacket, eyes on them, clearly waiting for her to start toward the stairs and the end of the evening.

Mario, quick to sense the unspoken meaning behind her half-finished sentence, said gently, "Ah, don't fear, Jennifer love, I give you my word, I shan't woo you

more than you prefer." He held up a hand. "I swear—
what is it you say in America?—scout's honor!"

Still Jennifer hesitated. One short week in this lovely
city, then she could be leaving, who knew when to return.
She didn't want to miss anything . . . and Mario had
promised not to press her. As for possible danger, that
was the least of her concern. After all, hadn't Scott said
earlier this evening that he wasn't certain about the kidnapping threat being serious, either?

Jennifer looked quickly toward Scott, standing there
with an air of overpatience, looking like a bored prison
guard. That was all it took to topple her into agreement.

"I accept both your invitation and your word, Mario.
I shall hold you firmly to your promise!" Jennifer's eyes
began to sparkle with mischief and excitement. "When?"

Mario's voice was still pitched too low to reach Scott's
ears. "I'll await you in the gondola as soon as you can
evade our friend standing by the wall over there. Slip
out to join me. I promise, I shall protect you as well as he
could."

Jennifer couldn't help another quick glance in Scott's
direction, then turned back to say good night to Mario
before going toward the door. Angelina had already gone
to her room moments before. As Jennifer started across
the marble foyer, she was aware Scott had resumed his
usual procedure of trailing right behind her.

When she had reached the door of her room, she
turned her head to tell him good night, only to be met
by a shrewd look in Scott's eyes.

"You're up to something. I sense it. What is it?" he
asked impatiently. "You've got that impish look. I don't
trust you."

Jennifer smiled. "You never have, have you, Scott? Not
really." Her voice was all honey and innocence as
she tried to control the flicker in her eyes. "Good night,
Scott."

As she stepped into her room, she caught a final
glimpse of him standing there, frowning, indecisive, and
suspicious.

"Good night, Jennifer," he said reluctantly.

The door closed behind her, and she leaned against it, listening until she heard him, after he had hesitated for a few moments, finally go into his own room and close the door.

7

Jennifer went over to the closet to get a soft white wool cape to slip about her shoulders. Then she returned to her door, pressing her ear close to it, listening. How conspiratorial and yet a bit guilty she felt.

There was no sound. Going over to the French windows opening onto the balcony, she opened them a trifle and peered out. The balcony was empty, though the light streamed out from Scott's room. Smiling a little uneasily, she reflected that this was a ridiculous game she was being forced into playing.

She waited a few more minutes, just to be safe. Then, as she was ready to leave, she was startled by a light knock at her door. Going quietly up to it, she whispered softly, "Who is it?"

"Just checking!" came Scott's voice from the other side.

"Good night!" she snapped tartly. The very idea! He was like a sorority house mother making a bed check! She let her breath slide out in exasperation. Waiting a few moments once again until she was certain he had returned to his room, she reflected that if he had knocked just minutes later than he had, she would have been gone. Worse yet, he might have intercepted her in the hall on her way to the stairs.

Suddenly the faint sound of water running reached her ears. Jennifer smiled. Scott, apparently deciding his work was over for the evening, was taking a shower. Opening the door quickly, she slipped out, heading for the stairway. Small dimmed lights had been left burning along the hall and downstairs in the foyer. There was no sound but the soft touch of her thin-soled shoes on the marble steps, and that was barely audible to her own ears. She moved swiftly toward the heavy front door and pulled it open.

Outside, the whole magic world of Venice night met her eyes. The moon spread a silver patina across the water, the air was soft with only the faintest of breezes stirring the material of her white dinner dress. The gondola bobbed gently up and down as Mario quickly stepped up onto the tiny dock to take her hand and help her to her seat.

"There, did I exaggerate?" Mario motioned a casual hand toward the moon-spattered silhouettes of buildings and church spires.

Jennifer felt her breath catch in her throat as she gazed about her, the borderline between reality and unreality becoming blurred. It was a city of glittering fantasy. She shivered slightly, not from the dampness of the night air, but from sheer excitement and delight.

Perhaps that was why she didn't notice another boat, resting nearby in one of the small shadowy canals, pull out to follow their gondola, moving through the night toward the city's center.

"It's all so beautiful, Mario," Jennifer said, her voice catching. "I wouldn't have missed it for anything."

"When the heart sees Venice, no city is like it. Yet there are those who look at it and turn away, saying Venice is dank and dirty, decaying, and it smells evil." Mario spoke with a shade of bitterness overlaying his voice.

Jennifer realized with a start that, for some silly reason, she wanted Scott to see the city as she was seeing it tonight. How ridiculous! Wasn't that the idea of this outing, to see it without him?

The gondola slipped out of the main canal into one of the dark waterways, the sound of the water louder in its slap against buildings close on either side. The boat curled in and out through an impossible maze of small canals, one so much like the other that Jennifer lost all sense of direction.

Suddenly the gondola slid out of a twisting small

canal, out of the gloom only infrequently laced with moonlight, into a brilliant display of lights splattering blue and red upon the water. There was a joyous sound of spirited music and laughter. In the small *campo,* people were milling about, dancing, talking, in a never-ceasing panorama.

"Shall we pull in here and join them for a while?" Mario bent close to her.

"No, Mario, I don't think so," Jennifer said, looking at the celebrating participants, who seemed to fill the small square to its very edges. "If you don't mind, I'd rather just float along here for a little while, watching and listening, then go back slowly along the canal toward home. We've already been out for some time, and it was really pretty late when we started."

He lifted her hand to kiss it. "As you will, Jennifer. See how well-behaved I am? Not because I want to be!" He smiled at her, his teeth glistening white in the brilliance of the lights.

After a little while they started back, the gondola edging slowly, almost silently, through the rabbit warren of houses crouching at the edge of the small waterways. Sometimes the moon bathed them in silver, sometimes the way was laddered with strips of moonlight and dark as they wound in and about.

Mario laid a hand on hers. "Jennifer, you need not go on to other places," he said pleadingly. "Stay here for four weeks, stay on here for a lifetime with me. I'm quite serious, you know."

Oh, dear, here it was again, Jennifer thought uncomfortably. Somehow she'd thought Constance might have served to distract his mind, but clearly she hadn't.

But before she had time to think up what to reply, a string of words in Italian came from the gondolier. Mario twisted back to answer, then half-rose in his seat, to lean over the edge of the boat and gaze back down the winding small canal behind them, peering through the moonlight.

"What is it, Mario, something wrong?" Jennifer asked

anxiously, a little flutter of uneasiness beginning to make itself felt under her rib cage.

"Just a moment," he said, then spoke quickly to the gondolier, to be answered by a few words.

Mario slipped back into his chair and turned to her. "Nothing, Jennifer, nothing to worry about. Paolo said he noticed that a small boat has been following us for some time; he felt he should notify me. We're not completely free of a criminal element here, much as we'd like to think we are, though it's a little hard to rob anyone from a boat. Anyhow, whoever, whatever it was, it's gone. Turned off in the other direction while I was looking," he reassured her.

While he was looking, or because someone saw him looking? Jennifer wondered uneasily. Then she shoved the nervous thought from her mind. Scott had her doing it now!

The night was no less beautiful as they approached the *palazzo*. Jennifer could have stayed out in this mystic dreamlike evening endlessly, but now it was very late, and the long day was catching up with her.

As she and Mario stepped out onto the small mooring and the gondola pulled away, Mario took her hand and drew her gently to him. "It is not much to be a count these days, but if you would be my *contessa*, dear Jennifer, I would serve you faithfully all my life. I mean that sincerely."

Somehow she knew he meant it. There was something in his voice that was deeply convincing.

And it made her miserable. "I'm sorry, Mario," she said unhappily, "I really can't—"

"Don't, Jennifer, not yet. We still have time, perhaps I can convince you that even if you don't feel you love me, you might learn to. That can happen, you know. If you cannot say yes, at least . . . don't tell me no for another few days." He bent and kissed her ever so gently. "That doesn't break my promise, that kiss, it's a . . . a friendly kiss."

He opened the door, and they went silently into the *palazzo* and up the stairs, Mario accompanying Jennifer to her door. Lifting her chin with a finger, he looked into her eyes. "Don't say no, Jennifer," he whispered, his eyes dark and amorous in the glow of the hall light.

She did not try to answer, but said good night softly as he turned and went down the hall quietly as she opened her door to enter her room.

Inside, she halted, startled. There, in her bedroom, sat Scott, on the edge of a chair, facing her, glaring, wearing a bathrobe knotted at the waist.

"Where in the hell have you been?" The words were no less sharp for being uttered in a low voice.

"What are you doing in my room?" she snapped back.

"Waiting for you to return. *If* you returned!" It was almost a hiss.

"Just who do you think you are? My father? Uncle Henry?" she said in a small voice that was beginning to quiver with anger. "Will you please leave my room? I'd like to go to bed, if you don't mind. What are you doing, coming in here, dressed like that? Out! Now!" She was so infuriated that she couldn't say another word; she pointed toward the door.

He ignored her comments. "You little fool. I don't know where you went, but what you did was stupid and dangerous. You were with Mario, I suppose. He ought to have had better sense." His low, angry voice swept on. "Someone could have jumped out from a dark place, hit Mario on the head, and grabbed you. The trail could be cold before we realized you were gone."

"We were in a gondola the whole time. A little hard to hit anyone on the head if you're passing by in another boat," she said tartly, finding her voice once again. Quickly she shoved the thought of the small boat into a far corner of her mind. Certainly she wasn't going to tell him about it. It wasn't anything, but no doubt he'd read real danger into it, and she'd never get to go anywhere!

Then she stared at him coldly. "Are you going to get out of my room or not?" She put her hands on her hips and said indignantly, "How did you get in here?"

Scott jerked his head impatiently toward the French

window. "That way. You left it open. After I got out of the shower, I started thinking about how you looked at me with those big innocent eyes. Too damned innocent! I put my robe on and came to your door. You didn't answer my knock. I first thought you might be on the balcony again. You weren't. You weren't anywhere! I was right not to trust you—you were gone!"

He thrust himself out of the chair, looming tall and angry as he looked down at her. "This is the worst damned job I've ever had, playing nursemaid and protector to someone who keeps acting like a stupid little fool! Haven't you got enough sense to realize no one's playing games but you? Serve you right if you did get grabbed!"

His hands shot out to fasten on her arms, shaking her slightly, his eyes burning with frustration and temper.

Jennifer stared up at him, dazed. She must be crazy, she thought dizzily. She didn't even hear what he was saying; all she was conscious of was the touch of his hands on her bare arms, of his nearness. *She wanted him to kiss her!* Confusion robbed her of words. She was completely unnerved.

Scott gave her one final brisk shake and snapped, "Now, let's have an end to the fox-and-hounds game, once and for all! I mean it!"

That he did. It was easy for Jennifer to see that. His gray eyes were hot with anger still, the line of his mouth was hard, and a vein in his temple throbbed.

Starting for the door, he turned to toss a few last words at her in an emphatic low voice, "You won't think it's so funny if you do get carried off. Guys like that aren't humorous!"

The door opened and shut quietly. He was gone. Jennifer stood where she was, unmoving for a long moment; then she lifted her hand, her fingers absently touching her lips. *She had wanted him to kiss her!*

Slowly she walked over to her wardrobe closet, like a woman in a dream. Small disturbing emotions kept trying to enter into her mind, but she shook her head, struggling to keep them out.

Venice. That was it. She would concentrate on Venice, the lights, the music. The moonlight. The sound the gondola made as it passed through the water with that odd little whooshing sound.

She wanted him to kiss her. She put her hand to her head, trailing her fingers through her hair abstractedly. Going over to her bed, she sank down on it, eyes gazing unseeing at the carpet. From outside floated the never-ceasing sound of Venice, the dip of the oars, the murmur of voices, and from somewhere in the distance the chiming of church bells.

Jennifer tried to battle against allowing her thoughts to circle about, constantly pelting her with the truth that she didn't want to accept. But she couldn't evade the hard painful twist of her heart inside her ribs. Of all the awful things to have happened!

Scott, of all men, to affect her like this! He'd been bawling her out, furious at her and showing it . . . and how had she reacted? By a silly yearning to have him grab her and kiss her!

She kicked off a shoe angrily, then the other one, and drew her legs up onto the bed to fold them under her, her dress crushing around her in a white cloud. With her hand she reached up to unbutton the cape, letting it slide into a heap beside her. For fully five minutes she sat there, almost motionless, upset, uncertain.

Now, from a passing boat, came the soft haunting sound of a man singing what could only be a love song, for it lilted achingly poignant through the night, gradually fading in the distance. Jennifer flung herself from the bed hurriedly to rush over and shut the windows.

Mechanically she undressed, shaking out the gown she'd worn, hanging it up, slipping the cape onto a hanger. Going into the bathroom, she scrubbed at her face and brushed her teeth with unnecessary vigor. But when she lifted her head, she couldn't escape the glimpse of her telltale eyes.

As she slipped into bed, flipping off the light, she lay back on the pillow. One thought gripped her mind. Scott must never suspect how she had reacted to him a little while ago. He'd made so clear how little he relished being along on this trip with her. She'd simply die if he ever should learn . . . *anything!*

Closing her eyes tight, she tried to force herself to strip her mind of all thought, and sleep. But she lay awake for a long restless period of time.

Jennifer struggled awake in the morning, only to face the unhappy thought that she'd be seeing Scott. Seeing him and not letting him catch the faintest suspicion about last night. Sitting up in bed, Jennifer scowled. She'd wanted him to kiss her! Indeed! How . . . how silly!

Throwing back the covers, she flounced into the bathroom to shower. Stop being so foolish, she scolded herself briskly. Don't get all weak-kneed and disturbed about what was only a moment of physical attraction! It could happen to anyone, temporarily, momentarily.

Her morale reinforced now, Jennifer showered, dressed, and started down the hall toward the stairs, telling Emilia she'd have her coffee at breakfast instead of in her room. Scott's door was still closed, and Jennifer was pleased to note she had been correct about her fleeting reaction last night. Smiling to herself, she decided it was purely a matter of seeing things clearly. Now the thought of Scott did nothing to her feelings, nothing. No heart flutter, no sudden intake of breath.

In the breakfast room, Angelina, clad in a stylish pantsuit of pale pink and looking as elegant as a fashion plate, was reading the morning paper. She looked up when Jennifer entered. "And where is your shadow this morning?" she asked, smiling.

Jennifer grinned. "Sleeping, I imagine. He waited up for me last night like an irate father. Mario and I took off alone for a little while, only it turned out to be a late little while. I had to answer to Scott when I came in."

"Was that wise? Should you have . . . without him?" Angelina set the paper down. "It would be terrible if . . . if anything should happen."

Then, giving Jennifer a rueful smile, she added, "I'm

sorry, I shouldn't presume to give you advice like this.
It isn't for me to say what is or is not dangerous. I'm
certain you're the best judge of whether it's safe to ven-
ture out without—"

"Not a very good judge, if you're talking about last
night," Scott said shortly, breaking into the conversation
as he came into the room. "Good morning, Angelina,
good morning, Jennifer." He met Jennifer's eyes with
the cool reserved look of a stern parent who was expecting better behavior from an errant child from now on.

Jennifer held her tongue other than to mumble "Good
morning." Actually, she had little choice, further speech
halted by the momentary struggle to remember what she
had decided only moments ago, that her reaction to Scott
was purely a matter of seeing things clearly. That this
sudden stifled feeling in the throat, the uneasy knocking
of her heart against her ribs, was caused by a chemical
action in the body, glands probably . . . or something.
Picking up the cup of coffee in front of her, Jennifer
gulped at it hurriedly.

It was too hot for comfort, and it went down the
wrong way, causing her to choke slightly, coughing, spill-
ing some of the coffee as she set the cup shakily down
on its saucer.

As she caught her breath, she inadvertently looked up,
to see Scott turning questioningly from the buffet, where
he was helping himself to breakfast. Setting his plate
down quickly, he hurried over to help her. Jennifer waved
him away, nodding, indicating she was all right now.
She didn't want him to touch her.

An instant later she really was all right, wiping away
the tears brought on by the coughing. "Sorry," she said,
"I just choked on the coffee."

One thing the incident had done, if only unintentionally, was to divert the conversation away from last night's
outing. But when Mario came into the room moments
later, Jennifer wondered if Scott would have the effrontery
to issue a stern lecture to him, too. He did not, however,
and when conversation began flowing easily about the table, it was only about plans for the day.

"Tomorrow I'd like to suggest going to the small islands of Murano and Burano, where we can watch glass-blowing and lace-making, in that order. It's required tourist viewing," Mario assured Jennifer with a grin. "Today, more of Venice?"

"Suits me," Jennifer said. "I told you I wanted to go everywhere and see everything. I still mean exactly that. But . . . should you . . . I mean, we hate to take up all your time," she added lamely, wondering why she had said it at all. It only seemed to point out the fact that he didn't work.

But Mario only said, "I can think of no other way better to spend time than showing you Venice." After a moment's hesitation he said, "I need a little advice from you, *cara*. My mother suggested we ask Constance to stay with us—she is in a hotel at present. First, would you two, you and Scott, mind having another guest with us, and second, how do you think your friend Craig would view it? My mother desires to show her own appreciation for the hospitality of the Hunters toward me. I suppose there is a third question: would Craig, do you suppose, object if he is not included in the invitation?"

Until now, Jennifer hadn't realized that Mario didn't really care for Craig. He had been unfailingly courteous and pleasant, but he would always be that, she reflected. Quite possibly he didn't think Craig worthy of Constance, and now that she thought about it, neither did she. Craig was amusing but . . . a little shopworn.

She hurried to give an answer after her instant of hesitation. "I think it would be delightful, speaking for myself. I like Constance. As for Craig, I think he's staying at a different hotel, so it shouldn't matter, really." Jennifer carefully omitted mentioning what Craig might consider a fair-sized drawback to the idea. Mario.

"You, Scott?" Mario asked, lifting a questioning eyebrow.

Scott was nodding. "I agree with Jennifer. And I might add, there's no such thing as having too many beautiful women in a household." He smiled at Angelina, who wrinkled her nose at him.

How carefully Jennifer avoided directing much of her attention toward Scott, lest she be betrayed unconsciously by an uncontrollable look or gesture, her inner feelings still too close to the surface. It was all very well to tell her mind that this was all glands and chemical reaction, but she hadn't quite gotten the message through to her emotions. That would take a little time, and it was up to her not to let him know what was churning underneath a hopefully placid surface.

As they left the breakfast room, Mario stopped Jennifer. "Do you mind . . . about Constance coming here? We really feel a little obligated. But I promise"—he looked deep into her eyes as he touched her gently on the cheek—"nothing will be allowed to interfere with our little time together. I've a lot of convincing to do in the next few days."

"Of course I don't mind, Mario," Jennifer said honestly. In a way, it might distract Mario from his ardent wooing of her, no matter what he thought.

Scott was standing, waiting, at the foot of the stairs. Heavens, Jennifer thought irritably, why can't he stop being so tiresome about this stupid job of his! And, deep inside, she knew she was reacting this way to cover another and more disturbing feeling. But she merely nodded at him in passing, and went on up the stairs.

The day turned out to be a dreamlike kaleidoscope of impressions for Jennifer. The six of them threaded their way through museums, churches, down narrow alleyways to go up and over the inevitable humpbacked bridges.

"Mario, I swear we crossed this very same bridge not five minutes ago," Jennifer groaned cheerfully. "Does it lead everywhere?"

"There are four hundred of these in Venice," Mario said in an amused tone. "This is not the same bridge we crossed over last. In fact, we have . . . let's see, about three hundred and forty-seven left to go!" he teased her.

Craig plodded right along with them, though he whispered confidentially to Jennifer, "I'm basically your in-door, weak, nightclub type. I keep reminding myself this is good for me, but I'm not very convincing." Then his tone changed as he gave her a curious look. "What's with the count and you, Jennie? Anything going there? Plan-ning on becoming Countess Jennifer soon?" The two of them had fallen slightly behind the others. Jennifer no-ticed Mario had moved up beside Constance, his head bent toward her. Probably extending the invitation to stay at the *palazzo*.

"Mario? Marry Mario? Of course not, Craig. We're only good friends." That should take care of any bits of gossip Craig was clearly hoping to harvest and sow, Jen-nifer reflected.

"Then you're really leaving for Florence in a few more days, unringed and unpromised?"

"I am."

"That sort of leaves the way clear for our friend Scott, doesn't it?" he pried, eyes sharp. "Don't mind me, Jennie. You can tell Uncle Craig—does your heart lie in that direction?"

The heart he was speaking of gave a sudden traitorous jump, sending a rush of warmth to her face.

Craig said nothing, but when she forced a casual glance his way at his obvious silence while she attempted to think of a crushing response, it was to encounter a knowing grin on his face.

"Oh, so that's it! Jennie, you're perfectly wonderful! Can you imagine the headlines: 'Millionaire Scientist's Daughter Weds Hired Bodyguard.' "

Jennifer felt sick inside. She'd always considered Craig a little gossipy, often amusingly so, and harmless. Her mind staggered under the possibilities. He was right; if he whispered the word in the right ears, there'd be titil-lating stories in those sensational newspapers and maga-zines in every supermarket in the States. Her father and Uncle Henry would be horrified. And Scott . . . ? Jennifer wouldn't even allow her thoughts to go that far. He'd be . . . he'd be . . . She swallowed hard.

Craig simply mustn't be allowed to carry away such a

story. Untrue as it was, no amount of retraction could ever erase the damage.

"Don't be utterly ridiculous, Craig!" she managed coldly. "You know that's absurd. Scott Mitchell is with me only because my uncle ordered him to be, purely for the matter of my protection. I would prefer he not be here. I don't feel it's necessary, but I had no choice."

"And there's no romance? Sure about that?" Craig was clearly amused, and as clearly unbelieving.

"Absolutely none!"

"And that rosy tremulous look of yours is not to be considered . . . ?"

His sentence was to remain unfinished, much to Jennifer's relief, for Mario had dropped back to join them, pointing out a restaurant.

"There we shall take dinner tonight, Taverna La Fenice. That is if it pleases you, Jennifer?"

Jennifer nodded quickly. "Yes." Oh, dear, that was too brief a reply, she chided herself, but did not add to it, still too rattled by Craig's knowing smile and satisfied air of being on to something.

It was late afternoon by the time they returned to the *palazzo*, and Jennifer had started to go into her room, only to be halted by Scott with a request to speak to her privately. He nodded toward her door. "Privately."

She tossed her head. "If it's about last night, you don't have to go over that again. I'm sure you said everything necessary." That's it, she told herself. Be brisk, cool, aloof!

He leaned one hand against the door, effectively barring the entrance. "It's not about last night, though I doubt that advice made any impression on you. No, this is something else entirely. Your friend Craig."

Craig! Nerves tightened like wires under her skin; her mouth went dry. Scott knew! Craig had told him . . . laughing . . . repeating his words of this afternoon. Jennifer wished she would sink through the floor.

"Well . . . do I get to talk to you or not?" Scott was beginning to sound impatient.

There was nothing to do but face it now, explain that

it was a silly misunderstanding on Craig's part, that what he thought was ridiculous. Jennifer sighed. "Very well, come in."

Tossing her purse onto the dressing table, Jennifer took a chair, lacing her fingers together tensely in her lap.

Scott remained standing. "I'm not satisfied with things. I'm uncomfortable," he said. "Here you are, surrounded by people I really know little of, and I'm supposed to be avoiding dangerous contacts near you. Apparently you have your own interpretation concerning Mario, that he's all right. So we'll let him go for the moment. Now, Craig Holman."

Jennifer's hands gripped even tighter now. She waited. Maybe it wasn't about . . . about what she was afraid of.

"I know you've been over the details about where you met him and how. But I want to know more. Search your mind. Has he ever been in trouble of any kind, anything illegal? What about his politics? Come on, give, go over everything you ever knew, ever heard about him."

Relief sweltered over her, leaving her momentarily weak.

"But I've told you everything. Twice. Everything I know about him. Honestly."

Scott looked impatient, and his voice sounded so. "I said *anything, everything*. Dredge up all items. You've surely heard gossip about him, I should think, anyone that is as much in the public eye as you say he is. Just let me have it all. I can pick out what I think is important."

"But, Scott . . ." She looked at him helplessly. "I . . . I just don't know what else to tell you. I don't have any idea about his politics, either. He doesn't strike me as the politically interested sort of person."

"And no gossip, not of any kind, not even a whisper?" Scott looked incredulous.

Gossip? Not about Craig, but by him. Jennifer shifted uncomfortably in her chair. The fear of Craig's talking about her began to seep back into her mind.

She managed to shrug. "No." Her voice sounded thin even to her. "Except . . . maybe about his marriages. Nothing important. Just that he seemed to always marry money. But that's all it is, just gossip."

Scott's eyebrows were pulled down into a sharp V. "Well, I don't get it, there's something wrong, somewhere. Take today, for instance, Mario asking Constance to stay here. Wouldn't you think that when it was being discussed, Craig'd have shown some reservations about it? He didn't. He told her, sure, go ahead. Why? Especially in the light of that interesting kind of friendship between Mario and the beautiful Constance."

Jennifer had been a little surprised herself that Craig seemed only pleased about the arrangement. Still, he couldn't really have acted otherwise, she supposed, not and be polite and urbane. So she answered, "He knows they're old friends."

"Yes, but who needs that kind of competition? You'd think he'd express even a shade of reluctance at thrusting her in Mario's company all the time, just in case! Not exactly the situation one would prescribe for the encouragement of one's personal romance." Scott slanted a look at Jennifer. "Speaking of romance . . . personal romance, I notice you've been a little touchy today. Has yours hit a snag?"

"Oh, romance, romance!" Jennifer blurted. "Is that all a man ever thinks about, talks about . . . romance?" Mario, then Craig with his amused surmise . . . now Scott! Maybe he was only teasing her, but she was in no mood for it.

He gave a low whistle. "Whew! Looks like I'm trespassing on some delicate ground. I'll withdraw that question. Let's get back to Craig. Seriously, Jennifer, I don't like it. Any man who has his eye on a girl like Constance, especially if he has serious intentions, is a darned fool to hang around us in the first place. Unless . . . unless . . ." Scott stopped and went silent for a moment.

"Unless," he continued after the pause, "it is somehow important for him to be around where you are. And having Constance here would give him the perfect excuse to hang around even more."

Jennifer rose. "Scott, I think you're dreaming up problems that don't exist, especially if you've picked out Craig for . . . whatever you think he's plotting to do. You thought the same thing about Mario. I don't know why Craig is acting the way he is, unless maybe he likes the chance to be around Angelina. She's as good-looking as Constance, so it could be he's becoming interested, and since you're bringing romance into everything, maybe they have a beginning romance going." *There, see if he could take a little teasing.* "Or does that bother *you?*"

She was unprepared for his reaction. Instead of showing anger or anything like it, he became a little withdrawn and answered stiffly, "She's absolutely not interested in Craig Holman, I'm certain of that. I happen to know!"

His voice was certain enough, too. That meant . . . that could only mean . . . Jennifer walked across the room toward her dressing table so he would not see her face.

"Oh," she said, her voice carefully expressionless, "that's a bit of news. I suppose you have a reason for saying that. Are you trying to tell me—?"

"Nothing! I don't think it's my place to say. Anything that is said should certainly come from Angelina."

Jennifer was stunned. It had only been a few days. How could Angelina and Scott . . . so soon? But her mind tormented her with the realization it had taken those same few days to give her her own disturbing reaction. Jennifer refused to call it love.

"I'm still concerned about Holman. I'm going to see if I can't run down a little background information on him." Scott was clearly severing any further discussion on Angelina.

"From Uncle Henry, I presume," Jennifer said, without turning her head.

"Who else?" Scott was brisk. "I wouldn't say you've been a font of great knowledge on the subject. I'm not joking, Jennifer, it's a serious matter, or could be."

There followed a stiff little silence before Scott said,

"See you at dinnertime. We'll be going out, I understand. And if I don't get to mention this privately this evening, don't get one of your bright notions again to slip out with Mario on a late date like you did last night. Stop taking chances!"

Now Jennifer did turn around, her expression carefully under control. "Please remember that I wasn't the one who hired you. I promised only to have you on the plane with me. I'm not obligated to obey you. As I told you early on . . . *en garde!*"

Lines of annoyance ran down the edges of Scott's mouth. "Jennifer Cartwright, I don't mind saying you're an unmitigated pain in the neck!"

With that he gave her a brief nod, and, going out, closed the door with a firmness that would have brought a smile to her lips if she hadn't felt so abysmally depressed.

Picking up her brush, she lifted it to run it through her hair, only to stand with it in her hand, staring at it blankly. She chided herself for being so absolutely silly, acting like an adolescent schoolgirl with a secret crush on the local football star. Here was a handsome, romantic Italian, hers for the accepting. And what was she doing about it? Slowly setting the brush back down on the dressing table, she grimaced. Nothing. She was doing nothing, letting Mario slip away without a second thought.

It was a rather subdued Jennifer that evening at dinner, though she made the effort to appear lighthearted. But for all her effort, she was aware of Mario's quizzical glance. He did not press her, however, and she managed to assume an entertained expression most of the time. But she could not restrain an occasional quick look toward Scott and Angelina. There seemed a singularly intimate air to their conversation with each other. Or was she only imagining it?

Trying to divert her attention and thoughts away from the two of them, Jennifer let her mind and ears turn toward Craig and Constance. Though Mario was teasing the English girl, Craig seemed to show no concern at all at their easy affection for each other. In fact, he was so much his usual self that Jennifer concluded Scott was only constructing straw men to shoot down. He was always suspecting someone!

Now Craig began to relate one of his wicked little tales. They all turned to listen to his droll recounting of the adventures of a famous movie star and her romance with an equally well-known name in the British House of Lords.

"And her husband was afraid of making a fuss about it, because he's standing for election in the House of Commons and he's almost overcome with a sense of *droit du seigneur*." His story would have been malicious had it not been tempered with wry humor and the cheerful manner of telling.

The only person who wasn't amused and comfortable was Jennifer, though she concealed her feeling. She felt she could almost hear Craig enthusiastically and slyly giving the terribly, terribly entertaining details about Jennifer Cartwright and how her father sent along a bodyguard and she fell in love with the fellow.

Jennifer tried to distract her mind from those disturbing thoughts by concentrating her attention on the patrons of the restaurant where they were having dinner. She watched the waiters serving Taverna La Fenice's justly famous dessert of flaming peaches filled with almonds. Mario had insisted she try it; she had, and it had been every bit as good as he claimed it was but her appetite had somehow lost its sharpness.

Struggle as she would to prevent it, her thoughts inevitably went right back to Scott, sitting there at the table, so relaxed, so unaware of the problem that absorbed her.

When she had been on the plane, she had made plans to rid herself of him at the first opportunity, because she resented someone dogging her footsteps, limiting her first taste of freedom. Now there was a more pressing reason. Though she fought against recognizing what that reason was, the uncomfortable thumping of her heart was announcing why. She simply didn't want to be around him any longer; it had become an impossible situation.

To be around him so much, often seeing him alone, and knowing that he and Angelina had already . . .

Slowly turning her head toward the pair, Jennifer was startled to encounter Scott watching her with a very queer expression. Almost as if he could look into her mind and read what was there. Her eyes darted away quickly. What nonsense! Certainly he couldn't know what she was thinking. That was her own guilty conscience bothering her.

Craig and Constance parted from the group outside the restaurant, the English girl promising to join them in the *palazzo* the next day. With that, the two of them waved and were on their own way, while the other four headed toward the dock.

There was another lovely moonlight ride home in the gondola, the mysterious city bathed in the same delicate silvering of the night before. Mario sat quietly beside Jennifer, his hand holding to hers gently.

Turning to her, he said softly, "Remember, I don't surrender all chances. We still have a few more days . . . and nights. Speaking of nights, can I tempt you once again? Scott needn't know." He nodded toward the dark-jacketed back in the seat ahead.

"He did know about last night," Jennifer said.

"And. . . ?"

"I received a stern lecture!"

"And so. . . ?" The two words lifted meaningfully.

"Not . . . not tonight, Mario," she answered almost regretfully. She'd really like to go, see more of Venice at night, especially by moonlight, except for one thing. Not because of Scott and his orders—certainly not! It was Mario, really. Whenever she was alone with him for even a short time, she was conscious of always being put on the emotional defensive, aware that at the first dropping of her guard, he'd slip through, pressing her to marry him.

It was a suspicious Scott who again halted her entrance into her bedroom later. "All right, out with it, don't try to con me with those big innocent blue eyes. Are you planning to try to sneak out later this evening again? Without me, and even knowing it isn't safe?"

"Scott! The very idea!" Her voice was all honey. "I wouldn't dream of disobeying your orders. Good night. Sweet dreams!" With that she pushed past him, opened her door, and went in, followed by his voice muttering something under his breath that sounded suspiciously like swearing.

There, now, she reassured herself as she crossed over to the wardrobe closet to hang up her dress and light coat, that was exactly the stance to take toward him. Breezy, flip. He couldn't possibly think that she was in . . . Here she stopped, her hand on the hanger, the dress trailing on the floor. She had almost said "in love with him." In her lifetime, up until now, she had never, knowingly, been dishonest with herself.

Mechanically she slipped the frock onto the hanger and back into the wardrobe. Could she actually be in love with this abrasive, impossible man in a matter of a few days? Or was it, as she had first decided, merely a sudden strong physical attraction, however temporary?

Edging off her shoes, she bent to put them away, her mind slowly circling around, closing in, forcing her to face what existed. She straightened up. All right, an end to this floundering about, nervously sidestepping the issue, she decided. She might, then, *might* be in love with him, as impossible as it seemed.

Turning about to head for the bathroom to wash her face and finish getting ready for bed, she realized that if she were truly in love with him, it was certainly a hopeless situation.

She hadn't thought she'd sleep, but sleep she did, deeply, without dreams, until a faint sound brought her suddenly awake. She lay rigid on her pillow, eyes wide, listening. There it was again, a small unidentifiable noise. Pushing herself up in bed, she strained forward, both to see and to hear.

Gazing fixedly toward the French windows, closed and latched now against the midnight sounds from the canal, she was able to distinguish, outlined in the moonlight, a shadow, slightly bent, as if trying her door. That was it!

There was that slight metallic click again, as if the handle was being turned fruitlessly. After a few futile seconds, the shadow vanished.

Jennifer smiled as she fell back on her pillow. Scott! Checking. He really didn't trust her not to slip out again with Mario.

Closing her eyes, she once again drifted off into sleep.

It never once occurred to her that it might have been someone else at the window.

8

———◆———

Jennifer didn't mention the incident to Scott next morning; she wouldn't give him the satisfaction of knowing whether or not she was in when he had tried the windows.

Constance arrived later in the morning, escorted by Craig. Jennifer was glad to see her, not only because she liked the lovely-looking English girl, but perhaps she might serve to temper Mario's ardor. Constance was proving to be a delightful person to have around, her patrician beauty made delicious by those frivolous freckles, her ladylike manner and dignity interrupted from time to time with wicked little giggles and a buoyant way of teasing Mario.

In the afternoon they all went to Murano and Burano, as Mario had suggested. Jennifer looked longingly at the glassblowers on the small island of Murano, watching them turn miracles of exquisite beauty in glass. She would have loved to spend a whole day here, fascinated by the skill of these people, but they still were to go on to Burano to watch the lace makers. There, tucked into pastel-colored buildings with their bright tile roofs, sat women in their doorways, their hands busy with threads they were turning into cobwebs of lace.

There was so much to see, so little time to see it all, that Jennifer's head was swimming with hundreds of impressions. They went so many places, they gazed at so much, there was a tendency for everything to meld together in a pleasant indistinguishable manner.

When they returned to the *palazzo*, a little windblown and weary, the countess met them, welcoming them

119

back, as she did each day, appearing like a gentle gray ghost, greeting everyone, always pleasant, always charming, but to Jennifer she appeared in rather delicate health.

One by one the days slipped past, until the week was drawing to a close. Jennifer had ambivalent feelings about her time in Venice. Sometimes it seemed as if the days had whipped past in a dizzying fashion. Yet, in quite another manner, she had the strange sensation of long familiarity with this city that some found so decaying and dirty, and she found so mystic and fascinating. It seemed almost impossible that she would be leaving tomorrow.

Mario had not one moment given up on his attempt to persuade her to stay, to marry him, beseeching her not to make her decision final.

Tomorrow she would be departing. Sitting before her dressing table, she opened her purse and took out the train ticket to Florence. Putting it back, she sat for a moment, thoughtful. Tomorrow she would be saying good-bye to the countess, Angelina, Mario, Constance, and Craig, and . . . if she were successful in the plan that was brewing now in her mind, good-bye to Scott, too. She never wanted to see him again.

This last evening was planned as a gala farewell one, and Jennifer looked forward to it with a bit of sadness. Even though, for every reason, it was best that she go, she regretted having to leave.

When she had finished dressing, zipping up her white cloudlike dinner frock, she couldn't resist hurrying over to the balcony to take one more look at the bobbing lights on the boats coming down the canal. Then, glancing at her wristwatch, she went toward the door and out into the hall to descend to the salon. There, right outside her room, standing with arms crossed, leaning against the wall, was Scott.

"Talked to your uncle today," he said.

"Again?" She lifted her eyebrows. It was becoming an everyday occurrence.

"Yep. Got a little more on Holman than I had. The

people your uncle hired could find no visible means of support or where his money comes from. Something's a little fishy. He needs money to live like he does. I'm going to do my best to see he doesn't plan to get more by swooping you off somewhere."

It was all so patently absurd. "I really don't see Craig as the devious spy and kidnapper in the employ of a foreign government seeking my father's secrets, nor in business for himself, grabbing me to hold me for ransom." Jennifer looked at Scott, then turned and went down the hall toward the stairs.

As she was about to reach the bottom landing and step onto the marble foyer, she heard a sharp exchange of words in the low-pitched but carrying voices of Angelina and Mario from the salon. They were speaking in Italian, but she heard her name. She was about to go forward when a hand grasped her arm, and Scott was beside her, silencing her with a look.

He stood, frozen, listening intently, his gray eyes alert. Then, motioning Jennifer not to speak, he beckoned her with his head to follow him back up the stairs. Opening the door to his room, he indicated he wanted her to go in.

Startled by the look on his face, she obeyed. If she had any idea of speaking indignantly, demanding to know why he had been so dictatorial, the words never formed. His eyes and the lines of his face were stone-hard.

"So there it is!" His voice was harsh. "Mario. I'll be damned. Mario, after all."

A prickling of nerves ran along under Jennifer's skin. "Scott?"

He stared at her with a strange expression of not really seeing her; then, after a slight shake of his head, he appeared to bring his thoughts back.

"All right, Jennifer, I'm going to tell you what I just heard. It concerns you."

She nodded uneasily. She'd heard her name.

"Angelina was ordering Scott not to do what he planned, that it was terribly, terribly wrong. That you

were too nice . . . too sweet and young. Too trusting."
He said the words dryly.

Jennifer opened her mouth to speak, then found it impossible, her thoughts whirling about, unbelieving,
shocked.

But Scott was not finished. "And Mario was saying he
was the judge of what was right. That what he planned,
he was going ahead with, and she was not to interfere
or try to stop him."

Finally Jennifer managed to say, *"What* was he planning?"

"I didn't wait to hear more, in case they came out of
the salon. I didn't dare. I didn't have to know more.
What else do you need? Isn't it pretty clear?"

"It's not . . . it just isn't . . . possible." Jennifer stumbled over the words.

"Listen, Jennifer"—Scott was all business now, the
executive in his voice—"it's important that Mario not
realize we overheard. All that matters is that we know.
We can be prepared. Right now he thinks we're taking the
train to Florence. That's going to have to be changed,"
he said firmly. "I'll see to it. But in the meantime, tonight,
and until we go tomorrow afternoon, I don't want you to
act any differently, you're to treat Mario the same. That's
important. If he suspects we're on to him, it would pre-
cipitate something we might not be able to handle, because he might have to act fast."

He gave her a straight flat look. "All right, can you
do it?"

Jennifer said feebly, "I'll try." It wasn't Mario; she
simply couldn't believe it was.

"Try? Trying isn't good enough. You've got to do it!"
Scott snapped. "Unless you want to find yourself in more
danger than you are right now."

"But, Scott," Jennifer said hesitantly, unwilling yet to
accept the shocking revelation, "there must be some sort
of misunderstanding. Mario . . . and Angelina—"

He cut into her statement sharply. "Angelina isn't in it,
and she doesn't want Mario in it! Didn't you understand
what I was trying to tell you? She was telling him he

wasn't to go ahead with what he was planning. Doesn't that get through to you?" Scott's voice was curt to the point of rudeness. He must have realized it, for suddenly he relaxed his brusque manner. "Sorry, Jennifer, I guess it's not easy news to take. I don't mean to bear down on you, but I sure as hell don't want you to be kidnapped."

"Then it isn't Craig, after all?" Jennifer asked numbly. "I thought you were so sure it was."

He shrugged impatiently. "This makes it look less like it. Unless they're in it together. That could be, too."

Jennifer walked awkwardly to a nearby chair and sank down into it. "I don't believe it. I just don't believe it," she repeated in a daze.

"Believe it or not, it's so," Scott said. "Now, it's time to go down and join the others. It's going to be up to you, Jennifer. We can get away with it, or we won't. You've got to act absolutely natural. Are you up to it?" He came over to stand in front of her, gazing down at her intently.

"I'll . . ." She started to say "I'll try" again, but smothered it and nodded instead.

"All right, let's go." Scott reached down a hand to pull her to her feet.

Strange, she thought foggily, everything was in turmoil inside her, yet the touch of Scott's hand closing hard on hers, if only to bring her to a standing position, brought a now too familiar aching to her throat.

As they went out the door, she steadied her nerves with a deep breath and said, "I'll be all right, Scott. If it has do be done, I'll manage." She saw him nod, but he said nothing.

When Scott and Jennifer entered the salon, Mario tossed aside a magazine he was reading and stood, coming forward to take her hand. Angelina was sitting on the long sofa, her yellow gown making her look like a beautiful flower against the soft forest green of the sofa background. Only a slight flush on the smooth cheek betrayed that sharp words had been exchanged.

Constance came in with the countess, the latter dressed in a black hostess gown flowing regally about the slight figure as she moved across the darkly glowing rug to take Jennifer's hand in hers.

"This night I am sorry to see," the countess said haltingly. "Tomorrow you go . . . it is to be sad, you are a dearly honored guest. Perhaps someday you return to Venezia and Palazzo Forlenza. But, tonight, is for *festa,* to make gay." She lifted her hand to touch Jennifer's cheek, and smiled.

Scott was wrong, Jennifer thought vehemently. There couldn't be anything villainous going on in this household. They were all too gentle, too kind, simply unable to involve themselves in such things. The countess, patrician and fragile, Mario talking animatedly now with Constance, Angelina laughing with Scott. Not any of them. He was wrong.

So it was not easy, the thing Scott said she must do. Even not believing, it was difficult. But Jennifer, somehow, some way, did get through the evening. Sometimes she felt as if she were two people: a disembodied one watched the automatic actions, the smiles, the lively nods of the head of the other Jennifer.

Mario showed no evidence of being at all aware that everything was not as usual. Nor did he slacken his pursuit of her, slightly gentled in the presence of others.

It was a rather subdued Craig who cornered her after dinner. "So you're going to choose the earnest bodyguard over the handsome Latin, are you, Jennie? You don't suppose you could encourage a duel between them for the favor of your hand? Such a toothsome tidbit for my after-dinner contributions."

The brash words were there, but the manner was not. For that matter, the smile that accompanied his statement was evidently forced.

"Craig, are you feeling all right?" Jennifer asked. "You don't . . . you don't seem yourself."

He nodded glumly. "Right!" He touched a hand lightly to his abdomen. "A little attack of *turista,* the traveler's complaint. I shall retire early to my bed of sheer agony!"

Craig couldn't resist making light of everything, Jennifer realized; it was almost a character role with him.

And she supposed that, in a way, his diverting and wicked anecdotes were his manner of entertaining those about dinner tables and at cocktail parties as a method of repaying his host or hostess.

"How long will you be in Florence, Jennie? Maybe I can talk Constance into going there, too. We might join you in a few days. That is," he added, "if I can pry her out of this fascinating household."

"I'm not certain how long I'll be there, Craig, about a week I imagine. Anyhow, hotel reservations are for that long," she said as she and Craig strolled over to the others and conversation became general. There was a lot of talk about regret that she and Scott were running off, not staying around to see more of Venice.

"Why, you haven't begun to see half of it," Mario protested. "How can you bear to leave without having luncheon on the tiny island of Torcello? It's a romantic figment of the imagination brought to life. It's mystical, idyllic . . ." He looked at Jennifer quizzically. "Am I tempting you?"

"Very much," she answered. "But I have the feeling that no matter however long one remains here, there would be still more to enjoy. So, though I hate to say no, I must."

As the evening drew to a close, Jennifer was still haunted by that strange feeling of being disembodied. In a way, it seemed as if she were looking on at a set of characters in a play. Herself included.

But she was not to escape Mario. As the others left, Craig to his hotel, the women to their rooms, Mario detained her for a moment.

"You worry me, *cara mia*, you are not well tonight? You are pale, and there are shadows about your eyes. Have we taken you to too many places, kept you up too late?" He gazed at her in concern.

Though her lips felt suddenly stiff, she smiled, a small rubbery smile that trembled slightly at the edges with tension. "Perhaps I am a bit tired, Mario," she evaded. "It's been a lovely visit, though. I've loved every moment of it."

Not quite every moment. Not this evening, knowing what Scott had said about Mario, not believing it, not really, but not able to put it from her mind, either.

"Jennifer . . ." Mario cast a quick look over at Scott, standing in his usual posture of waiting to accompany her up the stairs to her room. "It's quite hard, my love, to say the things I want to say, with someone standing near like that. Could we slip out tonight, one last time? I promise, I won't keep you out late."

She could not. For so many reasons. It wasn't that she didn't trust him, that she could imagine Mario was involved in a plot concerning her, yet . . . if Scott had told her the truth about that argument between Mario and Angelina . . . then . . . "No, Mario," she said slowly, "I've packing yet to do tonight." The excuse sounded lame even to her.

"You do not leave until tomorrow afternoon," he pointed out quietly.

"I'm sorry, Mario." That was all there was left for her to say now.

Lifting her hand, he kissed it gently. "Very well, my love, I still have tomorrow. Maybe a miracle will happen for me."

Jennifer went dully up the stairs, feeling as sick within as if she were truly physically ill. Now that she could lower her guard, confusions and doubt crowded her mind.

"You did okay," Scott said, pausing at her door. "Better than I thought you could. I guess it wasn't easy."

She stared at him a moment without speaking, then said wearily, "It wasn't easy. And . . . and I think you're wrong about Mario. I hope you are."

He reached over to pat her shoulder sympathetically. "I'm not wrong, Jennifer. If you'd been able to understand just what they were saying, you'd know, too. It's tough to have to believe something like that about someone you are in love with, but better to know now than later, when it's too late for safety."

She wrenched away from the touch of his hand as if it had burned her. "It's not Mario I'm in love with!" she blurted out, stopping just in time. "I . . . I'm not in love with anyone," she added weakly. She'd almost betrayed herself, she thought wildly. It was all from being upset!

Brushing past him hurriedly to go into her room, she found herself halted momentarily by his sharp warning. "No funny business tonight, Jennifer! No slipping out! Whether you believe what I said or not, you can't take the chance!"

"I won't," she said flatly. "You needn't check up on me by trying my door. I'm not going out."

With that, she went inside. For a moment his footsteps did not move away outside her door; then she heard him finally go into his room.

She stood, restless and tense, in the middle of the Persian rug, eyes darting toward the wall separating her room from Scott's. This whole thing had become unbearable. Of course, this episode between Mario and Angelina had to have some other, some logical explanation.

And there was Scott. It was time now to take care of that. Their train was due to depart at two in the afternoon. Jennifer's eyes grew thoughtful. She could simply step off one train and find another that was going in a different direction. By the time he realized she was gone, it would be too late.

A little later, as she crawled into bed, she had a moment of wondering if she was doing the right thing in shedding herself of Scott. The only reason not to would be if she honestly believed in the possibility of being kidnapped, that it wasn't the same silly rumor she'd lived through a dozen times in the past. Reaching up to turn off the light, she gave an impatient shake of her head. It was no more true this time than it had been all those others.

Skipping out on Scott was the best thing to do; there was no doubt about it in her mind. How could she bear knowing he was forced to remain with her, when all the time he had to leave his heart and thoughts back here in Palazzo Forlenza with Angelina?

Jennifer felt her eyelids sting. She loved that aloof, difficult . . . She gave an unsteady, wavering breath. She loved him, she admitted bleakly. The thought of three more weeks, being with him constantly, trying to hide her feelings, seemed too much to bear. She could not do it. She would not.

For a long time she lay awake. If Scott tried her door or the lock on the windows, she wasn't aware of it. She did not see his shadow or hear him. When, at last, she slipped into sleep, it was to be disturbed by restlessness, tossing, turning, pursued by uncomfortable dreams. It was not Mario who was trying to kidnap her, it was Scott, dragging her down into one of those dark subterranean prisons in the Doge's Palace, chaining her to a hook on the wall, jeering at her that she'd never guessed he was the one. Then he had gone, leaving her with the realization that the tide had risen and the water was beginning to come higher and higher as she struggled frantically to escape.

Jennifer awakened suddenly, thrashing in the covers, beset by the nightmare. Heart pounding crazily, she struggled to a sitting position. For a moment she simply sat there, confused, her heart slowing; then she lay back down, conscious it was only a bad dream. For one fleeting moment she let the thought that Scott might indeed be the one, that his pose as a bodyguard was only to hide his real intent, slip across her mind, then pushed it sharply aside. It was some little time before she slept once again.

It was after breakfast that Mario managed to corner her once again. "I've got to speak to you, Jennifer."

He turned to Scott. "I've something I want to say to Jennifer. If you still are fearful of her safety, I ask that you remain outside the breakfast-room door, where you can be certain no one can enter without your seeing. And no one can gain entrance through this one window that opens high above the canal." His voice was almost bitter.

Scott hesitated, giving a quick look at Jennifer; then, apparently reassured, he nodded briefly and went out.

Mario led Jennifer over to sit on a sofa at the end of the room. How she'd like to have avoided this, she thought nervously, but how could she? That look from Scott had been a warning to keep up her guard.

"Jennifer, what's wrong?" Mario gazed at her levelly. "Something is. There's been a subtle change in you, both last night and again this morning. Tell me, Jennifer. If it's anything to do with me, I ought to know. It's only fair."

She tried to avoid his probing gaze, but he lifted her chin in the palm of his hand and gently turned her head toward him, looking into her eyes.

"Tell me, Jennifer."

Her mind scrambled wildly for something to say, not just anything, the right thing.

"I asked you to marry me, Jennifer," Mario said quietly. "Perhaps you don't wish to. That's your right. But don't I deserve to know what's changed you so in such a short time? You're not there when I speak to you, not really, your thoughts seem eager to evade me."

"I . . . I . . ." she began, then halted, helpless. It was futile, she realized, to try to tell this intelligent, sensitive man there was nothing wrong. He would see through such a fabrication.

"It started last evening, Jennifer, just before dinner. Before that, you were still the Jennifer I knew. It was . . ." Suddenly a strange look came into his eyes. "When you came into the room, it was there then. Angelina was with me, we'd been having . . . you heard us from the hall outside, you heard us talking, what we were saying! That's it, isn't it? But . . . you don't understand Italian."

She felt her face redden, and she lowered her eyes so he could not read them. But it was useless.

"And where you are, Scott is sure to be. He knows Italian," Mario said slowly. "He told you. I'm sorry, Jennifer. If you had agreed to marry me, I'd have tried to keep you from ever finding out. I wouldn't fail you, Jennifer. I promise."

"*Marry?*" Jennifer's eyes lifted now to look at him, startled. "Your argument with Angelina was about *marrying* me?"

"Yes, and I regret your knowing. I regret it more than

I am able to say. I swear, if you had said yes to me, God help me, I'd never have given you reason to regret it."

Jennifer blinked several times, as if that could somehow unravel the tangle in her mind that his words had caused.

He hesitated momentarily, then added, "It is not unheard of, in my country, the marriage of convenience. But that is often without affection between the two parties. I care greatly for you, Jennifer. Even without your considerable dowry, I would have felt the same. But"——he shrugged slightly, his voice wry——"Angelina was against my marrying you for the sake of the family. She said it wasn't fair to you. It isn't. I only hope you understand the reason for it. But, believe me, I would have tried to make you happy."

Then the argument had not been about kidnapping, but about an arranged marriage! The realization staggered her. She'd been trying so hard to avoid considering Mario a kidnapper . . . and he wasn't! Relief swept through her.

Putting her hand on his, Jennifer said, "It's all right, Mario. I understand now. I wish I could agree to marry you, but, honestly, I can't." She turned her head to glance around the room with its air of gentle decay. "It was partly to save this, wasn't it, Mario?"

He nodded. "Yes . . . partly," he said simply. "I'm unable to save it any other way, I've tried. Nor can I properly care for my mother, who is not well and should spend time away from the dampness of Venice. Confession is supposed to be good for the soul, but under the circumstances, I find it difficult."

Mario took her hand in his. "Since you say Byron is one of your favorite poets, are you familiar with something he wrote in 1812 about our city? How prophetic he was:

> Oh, Venice, Venice, when thy marble walls
> Are level with the waters . . .
> What should thy sons do?
> Anything but weep. . . .

"I couldn't let our home slip back into the sea without an effort to save it," he said. "The *palazzo* has been the Forlenza family's for centuries, it is my duty and my responsibility to try to rescue it, by whatever means I could, for the Forlenzas who come after us. It is a trust that I cannot escape. I must not. But if you had accepted me, Jennifer, I would have devoted my life to making you happy, I care a great deal for you, as I have told you."

"But it is not love, is it, Mario? It is caring and affection. Not once, now that I think of it, did you say to me, 'I love you.' You are desperate but not dishonest. I'm sorry, I really am."

"Ah, but I am dishonest, to a certain point. I was not going to tell you," he said. "But do not believe it was only a cold methodical plan. I would not betray you or myself in such a way."

"I know, Mario," Jennifer murmured softly.

"If you had not heard us, if you had not known, would it have made a difference in your decision?"

Jennifer shook her head. "None. In fact, I'd be more likely to under the circumstances now, but I still can't say yes."

"Don't think ill of me, Jennifer. In your country perhaps you don't consider these arrangements admissible, but in Europe, sometimes they are a necessity. In my case, this is true. But let's part friends, may we?" Mario's dark eyes were warm and eloquent.

Jennifer slowly rose. "Of course, Mario. Again, I'm sorry. Perhaps you will find someone else. I hope you do, someone you truly love and who loves you, because"—she paused to give him a gentle, understanding smile—"you deserve that." Then, without thinking, she blurted out impulsively, "The one you really should marry is . . . Constance."

"Craig Holman," Mario said tersely. "Fortune hunter I may appear to be, and probably am, but I would not try to steal a girl from another man."

Jennifer started for the door, but turned to again put a hand on Mario's arm. "Thank you, Mario, thank you for everything. It has been a wonderful week for me. I wish it could have ended differently for both of us."

He put his hand over hers and bent to kiss her lightly on the cheek. "And, thank you, *cara*. I'm sorry, too, it is my loss."

Jennifer glanced up, to see Scott standing in the hall outside. He had witnessed that little exchange of affection, even if he might not have heard their words. She didn't care. As she came out, he fell into step behind her. Upon approaching her room, Jennifer attempted to get inside without becoming involved in conversation with Scott.

It didn't work; he halted her with a hand on her arm.

"Mario . . ." he began.

She whipped around. "Will you please stop talking about Mario?" she snapped impatiently. "I don't want to discuss him. You were completely wrong, he isn't about to kidnap me. I know! For that matter, no one wants to kidnap me!" With that, she walked inside and sharply shut the door.

Jennifer leaned against it for a second. Why did she act so rudely toward him? She looked down at the toe of her shoe, scuffing absently at the pattern in the rug.

She knew why, she reflected bitterly. Those moments with Mario, stirring her with an odd mixture of affection and regret, had left her emotional barriers too fragile right now. It would be far too easy to unwittingly betray herself to Scott.

Out of the jumble of her thoughts rose one impression, that Angelina apparently opposed marriage without love. Jennifer felt a tight gripping about her heart. It was clear that Angelina wasn't going to have that problem.

9

Jennifer finished with her packing before lunchtime. Making one last survey of the contents of her suitcase to be certain everything was there, nothing left behind, she closed it, locking it, all ready to go when the time came.

Walking out onto the balcony to take what she felt was her last long sentimental look at the city of which she had grown so fond in this brief time, she stood by the railing gazing out over the canal, the wind tousling her hair.

But the sights about her were not completely crowding out everything else in her mind, for she was reviewing details of the plan for losing Scott. Like her suitcase, the project must be ready. What she should have done, she reflected, was to have slipped away from him in that airport in Rome. She would have fulfilled her promise to her father, the only real promise she'd made, and how much heartache she would have saved herself.

Jennifer didn't even want to think about Scott any more than she absolutely had to. It hurt too much. Love wasn't supposed to ache and pain, to make you weep. She set her chin stubbornly. Not that she'd wept, she reminded herself sternly, and she wasn't going to, not even when she realized that today was probably the last time she would ever see Scott. Yet, there was no doubt that it had to be today; no use in prolonging the misery of being around him, knowing he resented this assignment, that he looked at her and thought about Angelina.

"Sorry to disturb your reverie, Jennifer, but I'm going

to make some plan changes, and I need your help." Scott had walked out onto the balcony from his room.

Whirling about, she was as startled to see him as if her thoughts had suddenly conjured him up. But she managed a bland face and a calm "Yes?" *Yes, indeed, the plans are going to be changed, but not the way you think, Scott,* flashed through her mind.

"The first thing to be done is to talk Mario and the others, especially Mario"—he gave her a sharp look—"out of going to the train station with us. And that's going to have to be your responsibility. If you have no strong objection, we'll go first to Rome instead of Florence. We can circle back later to visit Florence."

"All right," she said submissively, because the change didn't matter in view of what she had in mind. Then, realizing her docile agreement without protest might cause him to be suspicious, she frowned and said reluctantly, "If you feel that's really necessary."

"I do. If they go to the station with us, it'll be pretty difficult to change plans and trains, both. And I can't very well phone here for Rome tickets, just in case the walls might have ears. So it'll all have to be done at the station."

He leaned against the railing to face Jennifer. "If there is any plan for something to take place on the trip to Florence, then they'll find themselves with a handful of nothing. Once we elude them here, it'll be a lot more difficult to pick up our trail."

Jennifer looked at him with a cautiously controlled expression. Scott still believed in that ridiculous theory about a kidnapping. Had anyone tried to kidnap her since they had been here, one whole week? Of course not, she reflected, but Scott had seen kidnappers around every corner, even in Palazzo Forlenza. She almost said so, but gave a mental shrug—what use in further attempts to discuss it with him now? So she merely said, "Very well, I'll try to persuade him . . . them, not to accompany us to the station."

It would actually be simpler for her in every way, she

decided. Having additional people present might compli-
cate her escape plans at the last minute.

"I'll do it, Scott. I'll manage to see we depart here by
ourselves," she reassured him, firmly this time.

"Good. Don't wait too long to get going on it. We
only have a few hours left."

It wasn't particularly easy to manage. Mario protested
strongly that he wanted to come along in case there
were any last-minute problems. "Our train station can be
an absolute madhouse with departures and arrivals. Since
no one can bring a car into Venice, many still come by
train. And, too, many do prefer the train, so they can
view the countryside. So . . ."

Jennifer shook her head, saying she'd much rather say
farewell here in the *palazzo*, where she'd had such a
lovely visit, than at the station, surrounded by shoving
crowds.

Reluctantly, grudgingly, Mario finally gave way, but
insisted the gondolier deliver them to the station.

Farewell, when it came, was not easy. Jennifer's heart
really did feel tremulous at the leaving; they had all
been so wonderfully kind to her. As they stood in the
salon, surrounded by everyone but Craig, she and Scott
joined in toasts to one and all with a glass of Punt e Mes,
even the countess, who shook her head at tea, saying she
wished to join in gratitude for the visit.

Craig phoned his farewell to Jennifer. "Sorry I can't
be there to deliver a bon-voyage basket of fruit . . . ugh
. . . food . . . I'm dying! I'm crawling back into bed this
minute for all day!"

As they were waiting for suitcases to be brought down,
Jennifer saw Scott take the hand of Angelina, say something to her; then she smiled and reached up to kiss him
on the cheek, sending a small aching pain under Jennifer's ribs.

On the way to the door, Mario spoke quietly to Jennifer—"I wish the miracle could have happened for us"
—then lifted her hand to kiss it.

The entire group crowded at the doorway to see Jennifer and Scott step out onto the small landing and into

the waiting black gondola. This time it was Scott who took the richly cushioned seat beside Jennifer.

Mario came out onto the landing. "Paolo will take you to the train station, but I still wish you'd allow me to go along."

"Thanks, Mario, but it's better this way," Jennifer answered, feeling that it sounded a bit inadequate.

"Very well, as you wish. Good-bye, then . . . better yet, *arrivederci,* for I hope you will return someday, Jennifer," Mario said; then, politely nodding toward Scott: "You, too, Mitchell." Turning, he said to the gondolier, *"Paolo, alla stazione!"*

There was a chorus of good-byes as the gondola pulled away into the center of the Grand Canal. Jennifer twisted around, half-kneeling on the seat to wave at Mario, still standing on the landing, watching them go. Then, when distance made it improbable that he could still see her waving, Jennifer slipped back into her chair.

"All right, that much accomplished!" There was satisfaction in Scott's voice. "Now, if he does show up at the train station, we'll know my suspicions are confirmed. But we'll lose him or anyone else, once we're on a different train."

Jennifer made no reply. Why defend Mario to deaf and stubborn ears, argue all the way down her last trip on the Grand Canal? Instead, she averted her head, to gaze one final time at the beautiful decaying buildings being ravaged by the sea and by time. No wonder Mario was fighting his own valiant battle.

As she watched, the gondola slipped under one of the arched bridges, past glimpses of tiny market squares, the ancient domed churches, gradually dimming as unexpected tears misted her eyes. It wasn't because of leaving this strangely poignant city, nor even of leaving Mario, though it was partly made up of both. Jennifer realized it was because of the man sitting just inches from her—that was what brought tears to her eyes.

Looking away steadily, so he would not see her face, Jennifer knew that her heart centered on him, that she loved him . . . and he didn't love her. She could have reached out and touched him . . . if she dared. And she did not dare. Jennifer kept her eyes on the passing boats and the buildings at the edge of the canal until she had gained full composure; then she slanted a quick casual glance his way, to see him sitting stoically, eyes forward, face thoughtful, remote. And, she reflected, his heart no doubt left far in back of them in Palazzo Forlenza.

In the distance she could see the station looming up starkly, and as they drew closer, there appeared small boats, *vaporetti*, and motorboats, lining a platform in front of the building. Here and there a gondola was tied, looking oddly ancient and out of place and time.

Carefully their own boat snubbed into the landing, and in moments Jennifer and Scott were out of their boat, their baggage beside them. Paolo hesitated for a moment; then, after being reassured by Scott that they needed no help to get either their luggage or themselves to the train, he stood erect, lifted a hand to his wide hat with its scarlet ribbon in a salute, then began turning the gondola away and back up the Grand Canal.

Jennifer's hands clenched so tightly around the leather handle of her purse that her palms were moist. From this moment on, she must gear her private plans to what Scott was going to do. Watch for her chance. Mentally she inventoried: money . . . yes, plenty of it; passport, yes; ticket to Florence, yes, it was in her purse.

"All right, now," Scott said, giving a quick survey of the area, "let's go inside. First things first. We want to change our route. We won't turn in our tickets to Florence here, in case someone should think to inquire. We'll simply purchase two to Rome. I've got a train schedule in the things your Uncle Henry included—he thought of almost everything. But"—Scott lifted an amused eyebrow —"he didn't expect this particular complication, I imagine."

Baggage handlers were already on the dock, and Scott indicated their two suitcases to a short swarthy man with chocolate-brown eyes and a wrinkled face, who grinned at them cheerfully with a gap-toothed smile, then picked up the two bags and trotted into the station.

Jennifer followed docilely. Scott gave her instructions as they headed for the ticket counter. "Stay right at my side, don't go wandering off, it'll be hard enough to keep an eye on you with all the crowd in here."

Jennifer let out an audible sigh. "Can't I wait over here by the door?" It was done purposely. Scott had grown so accustomed to her protests over his constant supervision that he'd surely suspect a too-submissive manner.

He gave her a sharp sidewise look. "I wouldn't trust you a minute. You stay right here."

After an interchange with the ticket clerk, Scott turned away, back to Jennifer, and tucked the tickets in his pocket. "I'll keep these, both of them," he said smugly, grinning at her.

He glanced quickly at a clock on the wall. "Say, let's move! The Rome train pulls out just minutes before the one to Florence, so let's get a move on. Hurry!"

Jennifer's mind was working quickly, her eyes alert as they boarded the train. "I'd like to sit here, if it's all right with you, Scott," she said agreeably as they came to the first compartment.

Scott gave an inquiring glance at the porter, who nodded. "Okay," Scott said, "here we sit."

He didn't even ask why! He was busy directing the porter to lodge their two bags overhead. The man left the compartment, sliding the glass doors shut as he went.

Scott relaxed against the back of the seat. "We made it with no problems!"

Jennifer was frowning as she fished in her purse, bringing out a small gold pillbox. "Scott," she said, looking up. "I've a headache—from all the excitement, I guess. Will you get me some water so I can take an aspirin?"

How carefully and swiftly she had checked that there was no water dispenser at their end of the car when they had boarded the train. It was going to be close, but it was her one chance.

"Or I can go," she said.

"No, it's better you stay put, not wander around the train looking for water." He stood. "I'll get it."

He had no sooner slid open the door and gone out than Jennifer was on her feet, grabbing her suitcase down from the rack, banging it awkwardly against the seat and the door in her hurry. Sliding the door open, she gave a hurried look at Scott's back as he headed for the other end of the car in search of water.

She barely made it. There was a shrilling of the train whistle as she reached the vestibule and lunged down the steps into the startled arms of the porter who was boarding the train that was about to leave.

She gasped "Wrong train" at him, then stepped down onto the platform just as the cars began to quiver, jerk, and start down the tracks, out of the station, on the way to Rome.

Quickly Jennifer slipped into the midst of a crowd of people, hiding herself among them just in case Scott could have returned quickly, missed her, then peered out of the window. Waiting until the train had disappeared from sight, she stepped out into the open, set her bag down for an instant, and waved a final farewell.

"Good-bye, Scott," she whispered unevenly, then turned away to look for the train to Florence.

A porter had appeared at her side. "Madame? *Signorina?*" He nodded toward her suitcase.

Fishing in her purse, she hurriedly showed him her original ticket, the one to Florence. Glancing at it, he nodded agitatedly, saying, *"Presto, signorina, iss late!"*

He began trotting over to a train that stood purring on a far track and stopped at the steps. Jennifer, a little out of breath, followed. Confirming that it was indeed the right train, she tipped the porter and clambered aboard just as the conductor swung up behind her and the train began to move.

Jennifer was still breathing a little hard as she slipped into a seat in an empty compartment, her suitcase stored above her head. Then she gave a sigh that felt as if it had come up from her very toes and leaned weakly back against the seat. It was accomplished. All but one important item. She must send an alerting wire to her father; perhaps, too, to Uncle Henry—telling them not to worry, that she hadn't been kidnapped. Because, of course, Scott might not observe her warning not to call them, that her evading him had been on purpose and not because some person had nabbed her. She'd send the cable at the next stop.

On second thought, she decided to learn if the conductor would see about sending the message. Their next station halt might be for a very brief time and she might flounder around looking for a message counter. Also, there'd be the language problem.

Jennifer rang for him, and when he arrived, she was relieved that he spoke English, if not exactly fluently, certainly well enough that they understood each other. Of course he would see about dispatching her cable, he said, and as he took it away, with a generous tip that brought a wide, toothy smile to his face and a polite tip of his cap, Jennifer was able to sit back, relaxed. Now that was done, too. No more problems. If Scott should wire or phone back to the States, all full of alarm, there would be no panic at her father's or Uncle Henry's receipt of his news.

Jennifer watched the scenery slide past the train windows, the countryside sights flowing over her conscious eye, but her mind couldn't leave the thought of Scott alone. What would he think, what would his reaction be when he found her gone? she wondered. By now he had certainly learned that she'd given him the slip. He'd be furious, of course, as soon as he learned there was no cause for alarm. Absolutely furious at being tricked.

She'd never see him again. Ever. That was a door to be shut firmly. Of course, she'd find someone else someday. He'd certainly not be at all like that arrogant, managing man who was on his way to Rome. Strange, though, how a pair of gray eyes, dark blond hair, and the set of a pair of shoulders seemed to rise and blot out all her other thoughts.

The door of her compartment slid open. A thin, pale man with a long face and cavernous eyes stood in the opening, looking about. "Pardon, miss, is there an unoccupied seat?"

There was so obviously only one occupant, a single suitcase lodged in the racks above, that she could hardly say no, however much she'd have preferred being alone, so Jennifer nodded and said, "Of course, come in, please."

He thanked her and slid into the seat opposite and began gazing out the window. The man must be American, she thought; there was no touch of an accent. Strange, though, he had no luggage. She let her mind wander over contemplation of the stranger; it helped keep her mind from concentrating her thoughts on Scott. No suitcase, she reasoned, must mean he was going but a short distance, or his luggage had been lost. But whatever the cause, he didn't seem at all concerned.

Jennifer was grateful that the man made no attempt to start a conversation; he really wasn't the most attractive-appearing individual, with that dour expression, pallid unhealthy-looking face, and dull passive manner.

Turning toward the window, Jennifer watched terra-cotta-colored buildings with their red-tile roofs, and the ribbons of gray roads filled with speeding cars, pass by outside. Once the train stopped, but only for a moment or two, then gathered speed once more as it streamed ahead. The clatter of the wheels of the rails echoed and reechoed with the sound of *Scott, Scott, Scott.* She shifted irritably on the seat, shaking her head to drive out the annoying refrain. As her glance brushed past the passenger opposite her, she was startled to see his eyes fixed on her unblinkingly, almost opaquely.

He turned his head to gaze once more from the window as the train chattered loudly as it roared through the darkness of a tunnel.

As they plunged out into bright sunlight again, Jennifer returned her attention to the passing countryside, until her eyelids fluttered shut, opened again, then closed drowsily.

When she awakened, startled by the shriek of the train whistle, she blinked once or twice, still in that foggy half-world between waking and sleep; then her eyes flew open wide.

Sitting across from her, next to the tall man, was— she couldn't believe it—Craig Holman.

Before she could say a word, he gave her a flat grin. "Beauty sleep over, Jennie?" Pulling out a cigarette, he stuck it in the corner of his mouth, keeping his eyes steadily on her as he lit the cigarette with a match.

"But . . . Craig, I thought you . . . you were ill. This morning when you phoned, you said you were going to stay in bed all day."

"Miraculous recovery," he said lazily.

Why was he looking at her in that odd way? she wondered. Perturbed, she was almost afraid to think . . . but that was ridiculous! This was Craig! What was wrong with her, reacting like this, jumping to conclusions? There was another thought, a terrifying one, trying to crowd in at the edge of her mind, but she fought against it, trying to soothe herself with careful small evasions. Surely there was an explanation.

Craig was saying nothing, simply sitting there, legs crossed, one foot swinging up and down idly, perfectly relaxed, smoking.

"What are you doing here, on this train, Craig?" She had to fight to keep her voice level and calm.

He removed the cigarette from his mouth and smiled. "Thought you'd never ask, Jennie. Just going along. Or, since I saw you skip out on your friend, I thought I'd keep you company. How's that for an answer?"

"Where's Constance?" Jennifer managed through stiff lips.

"Venice." There was an expressionless look on his face.

Jennifer let her eyes flick nervously toward the man across from her, the dour man by the window, sitting by Craig. He had a newspaper unfolded on his lap but seemed uninterested in it, evidently more absorbed in her conversation with Craig, the deep-set eyes unblinking, showing little reaction to what he was hearing.

Returning her nervous gaze to Craig, Jennifer found him still completely relaxed and at ease, watching her through the blue haze from the cigarette he was smoking, smiling at her in that new and disturbing manner. She looked down at her hands while trying to marshal her thoughts.

"No more kidnapping scares, Jennie?" he asked sociably.

"No," she responded shortly, her inner uneasiness spreading now throughout her body, gradually changing into a sense of real alarm.

She had to get away. Maybe there was nothing wrong. Maybe Craig was here by pure coincidence . . . but she had to get out of here, because maybe that wasn't why he was here at all! She couldn't take the chance.

Starting to get to her feet, Jennifer said, "I . . . I think I'll go get a drink of water. See you later, Craig." Her knees felt strangely weak beneath her.

Craig, the smile still there, stuck his leg out, blocking her way. "Oh, no, Jennie, I don't think you want water. I wouldn't leave the compartment if I were you. Of course, I'm not you," he said blandly, "but all the same, I wouldn't go."

"But I . . ." Jennifer felt a sudden surge of courage lending strength to her legs. "I said I'll see you later, Craig," she announced firmly this time, attempting to push past. There were people on the train, the porter. Craig couldn't hold her here against her will!

"Sorry, old girl, no can do! I won't let you. My friend Max here won't let you. Will you, Max, old boy?"

The other man gave a flat, humorless grin that was only a thin stretching of lips against uneven teeth; at the same time, he was flipping up the newspaper with one hand so Jennifer could see the revolver beneath, pointing at her.

"So, you see, Jennie, more than likely we win the argument," Craig said cheerfully.

"You can't do this, Craig!" In spite of her effort, Jennifer's voice wavered.

"Oh, but we can. But remember this, Jennie dear" —Craig became abruptly serious—"we mean business. You can be a good girl, do as we say, or you can cry out for help if you want to. Listen to this, though, and get it straight. If anyone responds, that person is going to die. Any of the train personnel or a passenger. You'll bear full responsibility for the death, or deaths, if that be-comes necessary. We will shoot to kill. We're not going to be thwarted. So sit down, like a good girl, Jennie."

Jennifer stumbled back against the seat and sat down with a sudden jolt, mouth gone dry, heart thudding heavi-ly. Craig was not lying, he would do what he said, with-out any doubt, she knew it. She felt it. It was in the very air around them—threat . . . a tension so strong it was almost visible.

"What . . . what do you want?" Jennifer said in a voice so thin and brittle she hardly recognized it as her own.

"Oh, now, Jennie, don't be so innocent." Craig ground out his cigarette in the recessed ashtray on the far arm of the seat. "By now you must be perfectly aware of what is going on. But"—he leaned back, plunging his hands in-to the pockets of his jacket—"if you would feel better to have it spelled out for you . . . this, my dear girl, is the kidnapping you've been saying would never happen."

"*You?* You've been the one all the time? That the rumor was about?" Jennifer clutched her shaking hands together, trying to muster her courage.

He was almost apologetic. "No, I can't claim credit for that. I'm like you—I think that's another of your father's perennial scares, they come like the crocus in the spring." Craig gave her a foppish smile. "No, this is a poor thing, but my own. I came up with the bright idea that day at the Lido. We started trailing you, Max and I, whenever you got out without the bird dog. Unluckily, it was only once. We even tried a bit of old derring-do, climbing up on the balcony to bop you a little and carry you off. Un-lucky again. Why must you lock your windows, Jennie? So we had to resort to this. A little public, though."

"You're not serious?" she asked unsteadily, knowing all the time he was.

"Oh, I am. But don't worry, I'm your friend, nothing is going to happen to you, not one single hair on your head will be ruffled"—suddenly the voice held threat—"unless you make it necessary. Try to get help, try to get attention, and whoever responds will die, thanks to you. And one more thing, my friend. Max and I, we're in this so deep now, so dedicated you might say, that we'd have no hesitancy about killing you, and even ourselves, if it comes to that, rather than give you up or surrender."

At that moment the conductor came by, shoved open the door to call, "Bologna, Bologna! Next stop!"

Jennifer sat leaning back rigidly against the seat, mouth slightly parted, wanting to cry out, yet paralyzed with the threat that lay under Craig's watchful eyes. *But, the gun, didn't the conductor see the gun?* Her eyes jerked quickly sideways toward the man called Max, who now was carefully scanning the newspaper that lay in his lap, one hand casually tucked under the unfolded paper.

Time stretched out a pair of long torturous seconds before the conductor nodded and slid the door shut and went on. Later, Jennifer realized the man had paused barely at all before leaving, but to her it had been an endless frightening period of time as she sat there, breath held fearfully, almost smothering with fright.

Don't let him notice anything, don't have him stay, not even one more moment, just go, her mind had prayed feverishly. *He mustn't be killed!*

Her eyes moved reluctantly back to Craig. He was smiling approvingly at her, looking charming in his own jaded way, a little world-weary . . . and formidably dangerous in his very calmness.

Glancing down at his watch, a thin platinum wafer, he said companionably, "We'll be getting off in Bologna. Almost there, and right on the dot! Now we shall see what we shall see!" There was a new note in his voice that made Jennifer suddenly realize, with shock, that Craig was enjoying this! Apparently it appealed to a dramatic sensationalism in his nature. The thought was frightening, and Jennifer shuddered as she felt a nervous chill run down her back.

There was silence for the next few seconds; the man with the paper . . . and the gun, rested his elbow lightly against the window frame, his forearm slipping down to the hand that still remained beneath the paper.

Craig was searching through his pockets, then, apparently finding what he was looking for, pulled out a key and held it up, gazing at it fondly.

"The key to your dungeon, princess mine," he said jovially. "Only, I fear I can offer only a small building, not much more than a cabin or hut, and, unfortunately, far out in the boonies, away from everyone—but me, of course, and good friend Max."

Jennifer didn't speak, pressing the damp palms of her hands together hard, as if that would summon up her shreds of courage. Over and over she was crying in her mind: Scott, Scott, don't come, don't try to find me! I don't want you to die!

Scott, if he did find her, wouldn't be expecting Craig; he had turned his suspicions all onto Mario. Why hadn't she told him about Mario, about the real reason for the argument? Now, if he saw Craig, it wouldn't be with suspicion, caution. Half-formed thoughts tumbled about blindly in her mind; she couldn't think clearly, or plan; she was too dazed.

"All right, Jennie, we're coming into the station. Crisis time, old kid. Walk the straight and narrow. We'll get off the train, go straight ahead, then get into a car that will be waiting. We'll be right behind you. But," he said almost coyly, "don't be naughty, Jennie, or something bad will happen!" There was a ferocious gaiety in his voice.

The train had slowed, and there was a concentrated roar outside, of station noise, echoing and reechoing, filling every crevice of silence. Jennifer, prodded by Craig's voice, stood, her legs stiff and feeling strangely unlike they belonged to her as she moved toward the door. Craig took her arm; the other man was at her back. He had taken off his jacket, and it was folded over his arm, extending just far enough beyond his hand to hide the gun.

Like a person in a nightmare, Jennifer made her way blindly through the station, feeling as if she were in a vacuum, seeing nothing, feeling nothing, only that paralyzing emptiness now.

Once, her footsteps stumbled slightly, and she slowed,

only to feel the man called Max press the shrouded gun against her back in a way that to a passerby must look like an unexpected colliding with the person in front. To Jennifer, it was a prodding reminder to keep going.

A small gray-colored car awaited them. Max stepped around Jennifer to walk up to the auto, bent to peer into the driver's seat, nodded, then opened the door to the back seat and slid in.

"After you, my dear," Craig said gallantly, putting her suitcase up front by the driver, then followed Jennifer into the car, shutting the door behind him.

10

It was crowded in the back seat, crowded and stifling. The windows were closed tight, and there was a smell of old and stale cigarette smoke heavy in the car. Jennifer, sitting rigidly still, fought to overcome the paralyzing sense of panic that blocked off her mind, made it impossible to think clearly.

The car was weaving in and out of traffic, horns were honking, there was the grating shriek of brakes and shouting voices, but these barely registered on Jennifer's consciousness.

"Sorry this is a little crowded, Jennie," Craig said, still in that bright social voice that somehow was more unnerving than anger or threats. "Bear up, it won't be too long."

Jennifer fixed her eyes on the back of the driver. She could see only the thin shoulders in an ill-fitting plaid sport coat, oily-looking hair that straggled down from under an incongruous red golf cap. She had a moment's glimpse of part of his face in the rearview mirror as he glanced up and as quickly away, leaving her only with the fleeting impression of heavy eyebrows.

Why, she wondered dully, had she expected it to be the man from Florian's? She must think, she prodded herself, she mustn't let fear occupy all space in her brain. Taking a long steadying breath, she forced herself to relax as best she could.

Craig wouldn't get away with this. Even at this moment, Scott, finding her gone, would be on their trail. A small spark of hope began to blaze; that's what would

148

happen. Maybe he would get in touch with the police. With the police, it would be less dangerous to challenge Craig.

Then she turned cold as her thinking cleared. No one would come. Of course no one would come. How careful she had been to deny the possibility of a kidnap. That cable to her father. How often and glibly she had warned Scott not to be alarmed, not to look for her, because she planned to skip out on him at her first opportunity. They'd all be angry at her, perhaps, but not alarmed. She had played right into Craig's hands.

Her shoulders sagged; helpless tears formed in her eyes and began slipping down her cheeks. Scott had been so watchful of her safety, and she had been a fool.

Reaching up her hands, she furtively brushed away the tears. It was too late to cry, too futile. If she was to be saved, she had to save herself. Somehow.

Jennifer felt her fingers curl tensely on her lap as she spoke carefully and, she hoped, coolly, to Craig. "Why, Craig? Why would you take such a desperate chance? You could go to jail for life!" Could he, she wondered. In Italy? *She mustn't let her thoughts wander like that; keep right on the subject,* she urged herself fiercely.

He turned to her in obvious amusement. "Money, little one, money! Your old pater has a sackful, maybe even a bankful! He certainly wouldn't waffle at letting a little of that financial lifeblood be drained off for the sake of his only child." Craig couldn't have been more affable.

"Then you're not . . . I mean . . . no foreign—" she began, only to be cut off by a roar of what sounded like spontaneous laughter from Craig.

"Me? *That* silly rumor? Don't say you suspect me of trying to filch your father's secret secrets in order to blow up the world, or something like that! Oh, Jennie, of course not! No, purely and simply, this is for money. I need it."

"But if you were going to marry Constance . . . she has . . ." The words were squeezed out of Jennifer. She knew she would get nowhere by questioning Craig, not really, but she seemed compelled to go on, as if fearing silence, fearing that little thought that was beginning to signal at the most remote part of her mind.

Craig pulled out a cigarette and lit it, the smoke adding to the stifling atmosphere in the car. He blew a curl of gray-blue smoke into the air before replying; then he said, "Well, I had thoughts about that. Not so sure now, though. She and the Italian were hitting it off pretty good, which probably didn't thrill you completely. Still, you can't tell, I may not lose out. I really don't care, once I get the money from your father. Constance is nice, but not really my type, to be truthful."

Craig shrugged, the motion thrusting his shoulders against Jennifer, causing her to cringe instinctively. "I really prefer someone with more red blood than so much blue. She's a lady, Constance is, but I frankly go for the trendy kind."

Jennifer sat silent a moment. The man called Max, on her left, turned his head to give her that thin humorless smile, regarding her in a way that made her flesh crawl. She hoped she would never be left alone with him.

Jennifer considered an idea, turned it over in her thoughts before saying anything, then decided to take one last daring try.

"It's useless, what you're trying to do, Craig," she said, turning her head toward him and making the effort to sound perfectly composed.

Craig was looking at her idly. "Oh?" He raised his eyebrows.

"You see," Jennifer began, "you don't know what I've done, and what effect it will have on your plans. As you may know, or have guessed, I warned Scott that I might drop out of sight. On purpose, because it was annoying to have someone sent along on this trip to watch me, without my having agreed to it. I warned him because I didn't want him to get excited and get in touch with my father or my uncle."

Craig simply looked at her, no expression in his eyes or on his face, lifting the cigarette to his mouth, drawing in smoke and then letting it drift out in pale wisps. He said nothing.

She waited until the silence grew uncomfortable. Then she said, "Don't you see what I mean? No one's going to believe I've been kidnapped. And if you're thinking my father or uncle will believe it, I've one more little bit of information for you. I told them I wasn't. I sent a cable. Just in case Scott got excited and phoned them."

Craig tapped a long gray ash from his cigarette into an ashtray before replying; then he said, "It won't make any difference, Jennie. Not in the least. Maybe you did exactly that. Knowing your father's tendency to get up in the air about anything happening to you, I'm certain that you, as his obedient and concerned daughter, wouldn't let the old bird worry without reason. It was thoughtful of you. But it won't make any difference."

Jennifer pulled herself together to reply a little heatedly, "Of course it will."

Craig drew a deep lungful of the cigarette smoke, then reached over to snuff the cigarette out. "You really underrate me, Jennie. I can quite easily convince your father that I have you and that you're worth a fair amount in exchange."

Jennifer's conversation ran out, her mind dried. Leaning against the back of the seat, she realized Craig was right. Once her father was convinced the ransom threat was real, that she was being held, he would agree to pay any amount. Then Craig would let her go. Suddenly her thoughts trailed away in an effort to avoid plunging into an abyss.

But it was useless. There it was now, the realization that had been there all the time. Craig was never going to let her go, ransom or no ransom. He couldn't afford to allow her to be released. She knew him. Jennifer huddled within herself, trying to shut her mind . . . but she could not. Instead, closing her eyes, she had to give herself up to despair.

When she opened them again, she saw they were on the outskirts of Bologna, down a long road lined with cypress, then out onto another highway until they reached hills and a less populated area. Craig paid no attention to Jennifer's leaning forward slightly, watching past him, out the window. That lack of interest on his part was a terrifying reminder that he didn't care if she took mental notes of their route, she would never have the chance to tell anyone.

Completely subdued and helpless, Jennifer gave herself over to thoughts of Scott. It didn't matter anymore, if she tried to fool herself, tried to tell herself she was not in love with him, but only momentarily attracted by unexpected physical response. Gray eyes and his dear ridiculous huffiness whenever he was exasperated with her rose shiningly and hopelessly in her mind. Jennifer opened her heart now, admitting love. He would never know it, she would never again have to make the effort to hide it . . . nor would she even have the chance to. Her despair now overshadowed her fear.

Where was Scott now? Jennifer wondered dully. After he'd found her gone from the train, had he traced her from the Rome train to the one to Florence? If he questioned enough conductors and porters, someone could have given him the information. *If* he questioned them. Maybe, she thought bleakly, her eyes fixed numbly on the thin shoulders of the driver, Scott had called her uncle and received the news that he and her father had had word from her.

And as long as he was in Italy, had he decided he might as well go back to Venice? And Angelina?

Her thoughts were interrupted by Craig leaning forward to tap the driver on the shoulder. "Here, to the right, down that road." He pointed.

The driver half-turned to nod. "Okay, I do!" He followed the short sentence with a rattle of Italian.

Craig shrugged, obviously unable to understand the rest of the reply; then he relaxed against the seat as the driver went bouncing down a narrow unpaved road between two rows of trees, to pull up in front of a small stone house ringed by a tumbling rock fence.

"All right, Jennie, out you go, we're here! Not the Ritz, but we'll make do until the courier arrives with news from the gods telling of the arrival of gold!"

As Jennifer stepped from the car, she felt stretched

tight inside her tense body. Craig's almost explosive gaiety was far more frightening than his veiled threats. Reluctantly she turned toward the small house, Craig's hand on her arm urging her along.

A few urns of dead geraniums dotted the rundown yard, the front door was unpainted and scarred, and when it was unlocked and pushed open, it revealed a sparsely furnished room with a stone fireplace. The place looked as if it had been empty for a very long time, Jennifer reflected dully.

Craig crossed the room to swing open a door to a small murky bedroom that held a dressing table with a clouded mirror and a not-too-clean-looking bed. In the center of the room were a straight chair and a small wooden table scarred with stains and cigarette burns.

Craig bowed ceremoniously as he motioned Jennifer into the room. "Your boudoir, milady! Do take the chair, please, we have work to do. We're going to have to get a message, a personal message, off to your father at once."

He walked over to the door after she had uneasily seated herself as he'd instructed. "Bring it in, Max," he called.

The other man came in with a small case that he put on the table in front of Jennifer; he hesitated a moment, then went on out.

"A little chore for you, Jennie," Craig said. "We need a tape-recorded, heartbroken plea from you, begging your old man to shell out fast if he wants to see you again." The amused dilettante tone was wiped completely from Craig's voice, making him sound like another person, his gaze chilling.

Centering the tape recorder in front of her, he then dug into his pocket for a folded piece of paper that he smoothed out in front of her. "All right, now, read this, and remember, no funny stuff! Or . . ." There was an unspoken warning in his eyes.

He set his hand on the switch, but before turning it on he said, "Make it come from the heart—the sooner we get a response, the better for you."

Then he flicked on the machine, and Jennifer forced

herself to read line after line of an urgent plea to her father, begging him to save her, ending with the words, "If you don't think I'm in danger, and they mean what they threaten . . ."

Her head was jerked back with a savage hand, and a stinging blow across her face spun her from the chair with a scream of pain.

Craig helped her up, back on the chair. "Fine," he said. "Very good sound effects."

With that, he picked up the recorder and walked out of the room without a word, shutting the door behind him. She could hear a bolt being shoved into place.

How long she sat there, slack-shouldered, face pained, she had no idea. Time lost all meaning. "Oh, Scott, Scott," she whispered brokenly, over and over, "Scott, for God's sake . . . hurry . . . hurry!"

Then, lifting her head, tears drying on her face, Jennifer blinked stupidly. *No, he mustn't come, he mustn't! They'd kill him!*

The door was bolted, the one window barred, there was no escape for her. Putting her head on the palms of her hands, her elbows braced on the table, she fought against giving up to despair.

The door opened again, and she looked up, to see Craig standing there, looking at her, hands on his hips.

"Face still a little red, isn't it, Jennie? Sorry about the histrionics, had to take strong measures to get the right pathos. Now, I must leave you for a while. Got to get back to Venice to put in an appearance later this evening, apologizing for my temporary indisposition." He smiled at her. "Sorry I can't take back any message for you. See you tomorrow, after I pick up a car of my own so I can trot back and forth quickly. Got to keep an eye on my prize goldmine!"

Jerking his head, he indicated the other room. "Max has instructions. You'll get food, eat it, be a good girl. Max and the driver, when he comes back, won't bother you. If you behave, that is. And you can't con either of them to let you escape." With that he was gone, the door bolted once again.

Jennifer stared after him as if she could see through the panels of the wooden door. He'd be there with Mario and the rest, concerned, perhaps, at her disappearance. Would Scott be there, too?

She turned her head away, trying to shove everything from her mind. It hurt too much to think of how hopeless her situation was.

Max brought in her dinner later, some sort of unidentifiable stew and a couple of pieces of dry Italian bread. He didn't speak, but only looked at her with that pale leering gaze.

Craig returned the next morning, smiling, cheerful, and full of the latest news.

"Oh, they missed you, Jennie, my girl. Indeed! And . . . angry . . ." He rolled his eyes expressively. "Scott was, anyhow. I guess he got through to your uncle right away, and they'd had your cable."

"Then . . . he doesn't know . . . not yet, about my being kidnapped . . . about the ransom?" she asked hesitantly.

"Not when I saw them last. He and that Latin dazzler, Angelina, were going out in a gondola together, alone, last night, moonlight and all that. He really was mad when he came back to the *palazzo* to check if you were there. And when you weren't and he figured he'd been duped by you . . . then he had to console himself. Which it looked like he was doing!" Craig gave Jennifer a sly glance.

It didn't matter, she thought dully; a huge ache filled her entire body and mind.

"I really hate to upset you, Jennie, especially knowing you dote on him. But later, dear, later, you can go back to the *palazzo* and win him back again." Craig spoke jauntily.

Jennifer turned cold eyes on him, looking at him levelly, not saying anything, not having to. They both knew there was going to be no later for her.

He strolled over to stretch out on the bed, hands locked together under his head.

He grinned. "Mite hard, isn't it? If I'd had time, I'd

have gotten innersprings, but it was a spur-of-the-moment idea, you might say."

Jennifer rose from the chair and walked over to the window. It didn't matter if the bed was hard or soft; she hadn't slept.

Turning about, she looked over at Craig. "They'll find out, you know. You'll never be able to get away with this," she said almost calmly.

Twisting his head toward her, he said, "They won't. The money will be collected in the States. I do have criminally inclined contacts. I paid a man, a dependable guy, to be me, yesterday. Just in case. He remained, a big lump under the covers of my bed in the hotel, if the maid looked in. She didn't. So I was sick a good part of the day, to all concerned. I even looked a little wan last night. The countess was all for bringing me a *digestivo,* but I begged off. No, I won't be caught. I may be wicked, Jennie, but I'm not dumb."

Then he pushed up from the bed, sighing as he got to his feet. "Well, much as I'd like to rest, much as I'd like to enjoy more of your company, Jennie, it's back to work. Another tape, to dig in the spurs a bit."

Jennifer recoiled, but Craig reassured her. "No, don't fear, no more harsh tactics. This will be merely pitiful pleading. And to tell them specific instructions will reach them by phone from an anonymous caller."

Jennifer sat again in the chair facing the recorder and unemotionally droned through the printed lines. Craig frowned at first, then shrugged. "Maybe it's better that way. Perhaps they'll think you've been drugged."

Picking up the tape recorder, he said, "Off to the commute run between here and Venice. I may not be back until tomorrow, maybe with news from your father, though I suppose it's a little soon."

The rest of that day and early evening crawled by. Max had just brought in her dinner, when he halted, the tray in his hands, at a sudden cry from outside. Setting the tray down on the table with a clatter, he spun around and rushed out, calling, "What is it? What happened?" slamming the door behind him.

He didn't lock the door. In his haste, he forgot to bolt it, ran crazily through Jennifer's mind. Quickly she flew to the door, putting her hand on the knob nervously, and pulled it open.

She looked out into an empty room, but though she could hear excited voices outside the front door, she could see no one.

It was an impossible chance! Jennifer took it. Slipping quickly from her room, she edged along the wall, into a kitchen that was empty, then out the back door and into the dark.

11

————◆————

Jennifer began sidling along the side of the house, toward the front, knowing she had to find the road back into Bologna. Her hands pressed hard against the rough surface of the wall, guiding her, for the moon was not up yet, and the blackness pushed around her like a blanket.

As she reached the front, Jennifer cautiously peered around. A shaft of light illuminated Max and the driver, standing in the pathway to the house. Tense, Jennifer began breathing through her mouth, lest she make any sound, though her heart was thudding so loudly she was afraid they would hear.

But Max's voice was pitched harsh and angry. "Well, my God! Go check next time without calling me unless you find something! Lights . . . car lights . . . could be anything! I don't give a damn if you only thought they were coming this way. They turned off, didn't they? Next time, make sure before you come screaming about it, ya dumb wop!"

There was a sullen mutter from the other man as the two of them started up the path toward the entrance; then the ray of light vanished as they closed the door behind them.

Not even stopping to think, Jennifer stumbled wildly around the flower urns, bumping her legs, but, finding the gate, she was flying down the road, blundering from one side to the other in her haste.

From in back of her came a shout, "Find her! My God, she's gone, find her!" It was Max, voice strident, violent.

Jennifer's eyes were becoming accustomed to the dark, and she was able to make out forms of trees and bushes along the way. Instinctively she left the road and plunged through the undergrowth, falling in her haste, getting up and stumbling on, berating herself angrily that she hadn't closed the bedroom door behind her. They wouldn't have missed her so quickly. Now they were on her heels.

And close! She could hear shouts from the road nearby, and rays of flashlights streaked through the trees. She was wise to have left the roadway, she realized.

Plunging on, one knee aching where she had twisted it, Jennifer came to a barrier, bringing up sharply against it. Her throat paining from the great dry gasps of breath, her heart pounding through her head, she felt along the uneven top of the barrier. It was a low stone wall, dividing two fields. For a moment she leaned forward, hands propped against the rocks, breathing unevenly. Then she climbed over and went on in her hurried stumbling gait until she numbly became aware that the ground beneath her feet was growing smooth. In the distance she could hear the baying of a dog.

Jennifer scuffed a foot questioningly against the flat surface. It felt hard, and she realized she was on a road again. For a heart-shaking moment she hesitated, unsure if this was safe. Was it the same road? What about Max and the Italian driver . . . and their car . . . would they . . . ?

Before she could make a decision, she saw headlights coming slowly in her direction. Jerking around, she started to dash back into the underbrush, when she noticed the lights were high, higher than a car's. A truck, then? Cocking her head to one side, she listened with every pore of her body. It was a truck's rumble.

Recklessly she stepped out into the middle of the road and began waving her hands wildly.

The lights came onward until they were almost upon her. For a sickening second she was afraid she would be hit, but there was a heavy hissing of brakes, and the large dark shape came to a stop.

"Che cosa?" A head peered out of the driver's cab.

Jennifer rushed up to the side of the truck. "Please, help me. Can you take me . . . anywhere?" she gasped.

There was a puzzled mutter of Italian; then the door slowly opened, and a man got out, stuck his hands on his hips, and shook his head at her in the truck's headlights.

"You A-merican?" he asked haltingly.

Jennifer could see he was well past middle age, gray, the thick shoulders bent. His English came out haltingly. Trying again, he said, "Es-speak Italian?"

"No . . . no, I'm sorry, but could you give me a ride, wherever you're going? Please!"

His head moved slowly up and down, and Jennifer realized he was taking in her snagged, soiled clothes, hands and face streaked with dirt and tears, her disheveled hair.

Suddenly the nut-brown face cracked into a grin. Nodding vigorously, the man said, "Fresh guy? Okay?" Bobbing his head up and down, he said, "English, I know, great war. GI! GI soldier, he teach. Sure, you come!"

Going around to the opposite side, he opened the truck door and waved Jennifer in, as gracious as any nobleman. She scrambled up onto the seat as he slammed the door behind her.

As he got behind the wheel, he turned. "I go Venezia." Jerking his head toward the back of the truck, he explained, "Cheese, *formaggio,* you know!" Then he frowned. "Iss okay, Venezia?"

Bologna was closer, but . . . Jennifer hesitated. Maybe it was fate that Venice was the destination of the driver. Maybe Max would be looking for her on the road to Bologna. Craig's words rang in her ears: "Try to get help . . . and the person who responds will die!" Max had a gun.

She nodded. "Venice, yes, fine, thank you. I'm sorry I . . . I can't pay you."

Starting the truck on its way once again, he twisted toward Jennifer. "No pay. You teach words. I forget much. You help, I help!"

She nodded, for the moment unable to speak at all.

Sheer relief at her rescue, gratitude toward her rescuer, and a mind tumbling with emotions tied her tongue.

He pounded a heavy fist on the wheel. *"Autocarro?"*

Jennifer looked at him, momentarily puzzled.

He prompted her with a grin. "English. *Autocarro?"* Again he thumped the wheel, then flourished one hand around the cab.

"Truck?" she ventured.

"Okay! I have forget!" Then he asked, "Iss true . . . fellow fresh?" He was politely curious.

"Yes," she said simply. What else could she say, how could she explain, make him understand, with his unsure knowledge of English? The time for police lay ahead.

Apparently he was satisfied with her reply, for he nodded and said, "Bad guy!"

The miles rolled by under the heavy droning of the truck. Jennifer's good samaritan, seemingly delighted with the chance to learn more English, exuberantly plunged into the new game.

Jennifer answered dutifully, from the top of her mind, puzzling now and then at what he meant, but mostly she was able to divert her thoughts into what to expect next, when they arrived in Venice.

Would Craig be there when she arrived? Apparently, since he had said he'd return to the hut tomorrow. First the police—she must go to them. She didn't dare risk her own safety or that of anyone else in approaching Craig without backing and force of some kind.

How valiantly she tried to think around Scott, as one avoids touching a painful injury. But finally she could no longer restrain the thought of him, and once admitted, it flooded her entire mind.

Of course, she'd certainly warned him she would try to lose him on the trip; flippant and confident, she had repeated it. So she really couldn't expect him to worry about her. Angry, Craig had said. Probably. But, she thought bitterly, quick to rush back to Angelina.

So, little doubt but that she'd see him before long. The thought brought that familiar ache back again, pressing about her heart. Oh, she'd be cool, take care of the business at hand . . . with the aid of the police. Then she'd leave, to go back to the States. Somehow Europe had lost its appeal.

"Orològio!"

Jennifer realized with a start that the driver had said the word twice, waiting for an answer. She turned her head, to see him dangling an old-fashioned pocket watch for her to see.

"Watch . . . pocket watch . . ." she replied tardily.

Finally, the driver announced, *"Venezia . . . ah . . .* Venice!" he added triumphantly, pointing ahead.

It was growing late; the ride had seemed both endless and distressingly quick. The thought of the confrontation with Craig . . . and with Scott, could not but disturb her. They couldn't have been on the road over a couple of hours. Jennifer watched out the window of the truck as it began slowing, then headed directly for storage sheds.

The truck hissed to a stop, and the driver turned a perplexed frown toward Jennifer. She could almost see his mind laboring for the words as he began uncertainly, "You wish . . . where? *Albergo . . . pensione . . .* ah . . . friend?"

She swallowed, took a steadying breath, and said, "To the police station. Police," she repeated firmly. "If you can show me where."

"Police?" His thick bushy eyebrows rose high on his forehead. "Not . . . *albergo* . . . ah . . . hotel? Police?" he asked, half-disbelieving.

He looked so unnerved that she was puzzled, then suddenly realized he feared she was planning to report something on him—something untrue.

Jennifer shook her head as if to reassure him. "The . . . ah . . . fresh guy," she said, for lack of a better explanation.

The driver relaxed. "Ah, *si!*" Then he shook his head. "Maybe only fresh . . . not too bad guy!"

"Yes, very bad guy," she replied.

He gave a shrug of his thick shoulders, nodded, and said, "Okay, I find. Police."

Ramming the truck into gear again, he headed toward the dock in search of a policeman.

Things moved so rapidly in the next hour that Jennifer's head whirled. A policeman had been found; she managed to make him understand, with the help of the truck driver, that she wanted to go to a police station. After a quick glance at her disheveled appearance, he complied. In moments, a police boat was chuffing quietly at the dock, waiting to transport her.

Thanking the truck driver, after securing his name and address, she waved good-bye as he drove off, looking baffled and shaking his head. Jennifer planned to send him some compensation for his help, but she realized there was no way she could adequately repay him for rescuing her.

As the police boat churned through the water on its way to the police station, Jennifer forcibly reined her eyes and her mind. Just being in Venice again made her emotions rise too close to the surface.

A weary-eyed police officer sat behind the desk in the station that, too, had that faint haunting air of age and dampness.

His eyes, as the first policeman's had, quickly swept over her clothes and streaked face, but he listened politely. Jennifer was grateful and relieved that he not only understood English but seemed adequately fluent in it. Her voice, trembling now, began the story.

Carefully controlled disbelief was first evident on his long mobile face, but it gradually gave way to concern.

"This is true, what you tell me? And the man may be at Palazzo Forlenza at this moment? The count is well known in Venice, you are certain he entertains this person?"

Jennifer nodded assent. "He doesn't know that Craig Holman is . . . is a kidnapper. No one does . . . except me," she finished in a small voice.

The policeman glanced at his watch. "It is not early, nearly eleven o'clock, but in Venice one seldom retires early." Pulling a phone to him, he snapped something in

Italian into the mouthpiece, then sat back, waiting, his eyes on Jennifer.

Now the policeman was speaking once again, this time in a tone marked by polite respect. He must be talking to Mario, Jennifer realized, as she leaned forward expectantly. They were conversing in Italian, and she couldn't read the policeman's face.

He was nodding, a few more words, another nod, then he put the phone down to gaze at Jennifer.

"He's there, all right, your kidnapper, if that is what he is," the policeman said cautiously. "They've all just now returned to the *palazzo* after being out this evening."

They. That must mean the five of them, then, Jennifer thought, so Scott was there . . . with Angelina. She shook herself, straightening out her thoughts; she was being ridiculous—there were far more important things now.

The policeman rose. "We shall move cautiously. Count Forlenza will improvise means to detain Mr. Holman until we arrive there. Meantime, a call to the United States, to determine if the tape you spoke of has been delivered, if demands have been made."

And to check on me, Jennifer reflected. But if they called from the police station, her father would really be alarmed. He'd no doubt had her cable, which probably irked him, but this would cause him to be upset, and be a confirmation of his longtime fears. Perhaps if she explained to the policeman, the call needn't be made.

She tried, but though the man was polite, listening to her courteously, she knew she had not convinced him.

"If you really must call," Jennifer asked, "please do reassure my father that I'm quite all right, unhurt. He will be worried."

"Perhaps you would like to tell him that yourself, Miss Cartwright, as soon as we converse with him." He rose. "If you will wait here a few moments . . . please."

Jennifer quite well understood why the initial call was being made out of her hearing. Surely Mario had confirmed who she was, that he knew her, and she wasn't perpetrating some kind of hoax. Then she realized that this was now going through official channels and would be conducted the way the police decided.

But she did not look forward to a conversation with her father at this moment. She knew that when he was called, no amount of reassuring by the police would calm him. Nor would she be able to. She could never reason with him on this subject.

She was right. He sputtered excitedly at her when she was called to the phone to speak to him.

"You didn't believe me, that there was a rumor about kidnapping! Why did you think Henry sent along someone to protect you? Where is he, anyhow? Why didn't he stop this from happening?" The questions showered on her rapidly, delivered in a keyed-up voice. "And what about that cable you sent me . . . or were you the one who sent it?"

Jennifer tried to explain between the burst of questions. "The cable, yes, I sent it, so you wouldn't worry. I know, I know, but I didn't want him tagging along everywhere."

The voice at the other end of the wire crackled. She held the phone patiently. "But, Father, this didn't happen because of the plot or rumor. He, I mean Craig Holman, got the idea suddenly, because he heard of the rumor. And I don't know where Scott Mitchell is. I think he's at the Forlenzas'."

She nodded automatically, like punctuations between his questions and orders. Finally she was able to hand the phone back to the policeman, meeting a certain amount of understanding in his eyes.

"He was agitated," the man said. A masterful understatement, Jennifer decided.

"Am I to be allowed to accompany you when you go to Palazzo Forlenza?" Jennifer wasn't certain if she actually wanted to go along or not. She wavered in her mind. Perhaps she would be needed to formally identify Craig as her kidnapper. But she didn't want to see Scott. Not ever, ever again! The very thought of him made her go infuriatingly weak inside.

But she needn't have been concerned about a choice,

for the firm official courtesy was being displayed again. The policeman said, "It is better you remain here for the moment. Besides, I have already dispatched men to the *palazzo.*"

Coffee was brought to her; there was a definite effort to make her comfortable while she waited. Jennifer took a few moments to try to improve her appearance, tugged rather hopelessly at her snagged and dirty clothes, washed her face, and brushed at her hair with dampened hands. Her purse and toilet articles were in that hut back there near Bologna. Staring at herself in the small mirror above the washstand, she found she looked exactly as she felt, weary, strained, and bearing the remnants of the uncertainty and fear of the hours past. No, she repeated to herself again, she didn't want to see Scott. Or have Scott see her.

Jennifer was restlessly turning the pages of a magazine while she awaited news, when her head suddenly lifted at the sound of voices in the other room. Startled, she got to her feet. Mario!

Rushing to the door, she saw he was talking to the policeman who had questioned her.

"Mario!" she called impulsively.

He spun around, rushing over to her; he lifted her hand to kiss it. *"Cara,* I was looking for you. This is a terrible thing to have happened! We were all shocked by the news of your abduction!" His dark eyes were concerned. "Craig . . . he did not harm you, Jennifer?"

"No, Mario. Not really. I was a little scared is all. I was afraid of what could happen. Once it was started, he couldn't afford to let me go, you know," she said in a taut voice. Jennifer didn't explain why Craig couldn't allow her to be released if the ransom were paid. It wasn't necessary. She could see that Mario understood by the way his mouth grew grim.

"Thank God you're safe!" he breathed.

"But, Craig, what has happened to him, where is he, was he still there at the *palazzo* when the police came?" she asked, her eyes shifting involuntarily to the policeman who stood watching them.

He walked over to speak to them. "The man is now in our custody, Miss Cartwright. There was no problem, he offered no resistance."

She felt relieved at that; at least the Forlenzas had been spared what could have been a distressing scene.

Mario spoke a few quick phrases to the officer, his voice lifting questioningly. The other man listened, replied with a nod of his head, and added a few words. They were speaking Italian, and Jennifer looked from one to the other when she caught the sound of her name.

Mario turned to her. "Sergeant Mancini has given me permission to take you back with me to the *palazzo*, Jennifer. We may leave right away."

Jennifer hesitated. Something inside her rebelled at the thought of going back there now. She had run away from Scott, to end the misery of being with him, loving him, and knowing he not only didn't return that love or wish to be with her, but had chosen Angelina.

Mario was gazing at her, puzzled. "But, of course you must come. Surely you don't wish to remain here!"

He was right, she thought reluctantly. Of course she didn't want to stay here, she hadn't planned to. For that matter, she wasn't exactly sure of what she should do.

Then, belatedly, she said, "Yes, of course, thank you, Mario." Turning to the policeman, she told him she would be available if they needed her for anything further.

Sergeant Mancini bowed. "No doubt there will be more questions, if you will oblige, please. Count Forlenza informs me you will be staying at the *palazzo*."

But no longer than I have to, she thought. "Thank you for helping me, Sergeant," she said, then asked abruptly, "What will happen to him . . . to Craig Holman?"

An official noncommittal mask dropped over the policeman's face. "That is to be seen, to be determined, Miss Cartwright. There is much investigation to be done. The charge is a grave one. We have yet to locate the others who held you prisoner, who were accomplices."

He walked to the room door with them, bowing them

out and saying good night. Mario and Jennifer went on down the hall, out the building entrance, and boarded a boat at the small landing, without a word being exchanged between them.

Then, as the boat pulled away, heading down one of the canals toward the *palazzo*, Mario broke the silence. "You have had a trying time, haven't you, Jennifer? Do you feel like talking about it now, or would you rather not?"

"I . . ." Jennifer paused; the emotional impact of all that had happened suddenly caught up with her. It had been different telling the sergeant, objective, guided by official questioning. Now, with Mario beside her, one who knew all those involved, except Max and the driver, of course, it was suddenly difficult. To talk about Craig and . . . Scott.

Then she said slowly, "It was my fault, really, that it happened. If I had gone along with Scott, then Craig would have been on the train to Florence, looking for me and not finding me. But . . . but . . . I left the Rome train."

Bit by bit, she told him, often haltingly. Now the probability of her death, had she not escaped, began to seep into her mind more and more, and her voice became thin and uneven.

"Don't be afraid anymore, *cara*," Mario said soothingly, taking her hand in his gently. "It's over."

She wanted to ask him about Scott, what he had said when he had come back to the *palazzo*, but there was no time, they were already pulling up to the landing outside the *palazzo*.

Mario helped her out, and she stood for a moment in the moonlight while he got the key from his pocket to unlock the door. The brilliance of the night about her made her remember the utter blackness outside that stone house when she had escaped, and she shivered.

"You're cold!" Mario had turned after opening the door.

"No," she said hurriedly, "I'm all right." She didn't feel all right, though. The thought of having to encounter

Scott again made her wish she could call back the boat that was already pulling away. But that was impossible, so she gave Mario a trembling smile meant to reassure him, and went inside.

The sound of the door opening must have signaled those inside, for Angelina, her mother, and Constance came hurrying out into the hall, their faces worried.

The countess, pale and distraught, touched a hand to Jennifer's arm. "My dear, my dear . . ." Then her grasp of English deserted her, and she trailed off in words of Italian.

Now it was Jennifer who did the consoling. "Please don't worry, Countess Forlenza, I'm quite all right, I really am. It's good to be back here with all of you." *But where was Scott?*

Constance, subdued, quieter than usual, must have been feeling the shock about Craig, but she didn't show it, as she, too, was solicitous over Jennifer's well-being.

"Scott didn't find you, then?" she asked.

Jennifer was confused. "You mean he's not here?"

Mario shook his head. "Not since you left, the two of you, but he's called several times. Angelina talked to him the first time, and I have since."

They were all seated in the salon now, and Emilia, the servant, came in with a tea tray, trundling it in front of her.

Mario gave a quick look at the things on the tray, nodded approvingly, and thanked Emilia, who gave a duck of her head and went out.

"Very well, now, you shall have some coffee and a good lacing of brandy!" he said firmly, looking at Jennifer as he picked up a cup.

She started to protest, but he shook his head, smiling down at her. "Purely medicinal! If I might say so, you look a bit shattered. Brandy will help."

No one questioned her further while she took a small hesitant sip of the hot heady liquid and felt it warm her throat, spreading like a soft cloud of comfort all through her.

She looked up over the rim of the cup. "Where is

Scott now? Do you know? Did he say anything about . . .
my vanishing?"

A momentary grin spread over Mario's face. "Did he?
He did indeed! I must say, he was more than a little un-
happy with you right at the moment. Wouldn't you say,
Angelina?"

The girl agreed. "Yes, but at the time, of course, he
didn't know . . . not then!" she said. Her eyebrows lifted.
"Maybe he doesn't know, even now!"

"He didn't say where he was going, what he was going
to do?" Jennifer asked.

They looked at each other and shook their heads. "He
simply asked if you were here," Mario said. "That was
some time after you left. Perhaps at the first station stop.
Then he called today again. Ah . . . he wasn't in the best
of moods, I gather. He'd apparently been talking to your
uncle, who said there'd been a cable from you."

"Would he have gone on to Rome?" asked Angelina
thoughtfully. "He may call again, though he didn't say
whether he would or not, did he, Mario?"

No, Mario replied, he hadn't. Nor had he said where
he was calling from.

A little silence fell. So that was that, Jennifer thought.
She wasn't going to have to see him again. And she
wondered why the thought didn't make her feel happier,
relieved. But even as that slipped through her mind, she
chastised herself for even permitting it room. Of course
she felt much better at the reprieve!

To turn the subject away from Scott, she asked them
something that had been worrying her. "When they came,
the police, what did Craig do? The sergeant said he offered no resistance."

"He didn't," Mario said. "It was strange. I think he
knew the moment the police came into the room. After
they spoke to him, not more than a half-dozen sentences,
he simply turned around and, in that light casual manner
of his, he thanked us for the evening and the dinner, then
gave us a funny rueful smile and said, 'Well, no one's perfect!' "

Even after everything that had happened, Jennifer felt

a tug of something close to regret over what Craig was going to have to face. He'd been an amusing, entertaining friend over the past few years. The one who had kidnapped and threatened her didn't seem the same Craig at all.

The countess rose and asked to be excused. Passing Jennifer, she bent and kissed her lightly on the cheek. "Good night, Jennifer. It is good you be back and safe." Then she left to go up to her room.

Again Jennifer had to recount the story of her kidnapping, but she had managed to get halfway through it, saying that Craig had told her Scott had come back, when the sharp ringing of the phone summoned Mario from the room.

"But why would Craig say that, when it wasn't true?" Angelina looked puzzled.

To destroy her morale as much as he could, to let her feel abandoned by everyone, Jennifer knew. To taunt her a bit about Scott's interest in Angelina. But she couldn't say that, so she shrugged and said, "Part of his plan, I suppose."

Mario was back. "Jennifer, that was Scott. He was in Bologna, at the police station. They'd just had a call from our police here in Venice with instructions to pick up the other two men at the place you were held."

"Police station?" Jennifer faltered. "In Bologna? But how on earth did he know to go there? How'd he find out about the kidnapping, that we left the train in Bologna?" She stared up at Mario, eyes wide, hands gone suddenly rigid by her side, palms pressing down on the covering of the sofa.

"He didn't elaborate," Mario replied. "He asked if you were here, if you were all right. The rest, you must ask him yourself, I'm afraid, for he rang off immediately after being assured you were unharmed."

"I . . . I ask him . . . but . . ." Jennifer stammered, "but, how can I?"

Mario smiled at her, and she could swear there was a flicker of amusement deep in those dark eyes.

"He'll be back here tomorrow morning," he said.

12

Jennifer smiled mechanically. "Good," she said, "I'm anxious to know what happened from his end." There now, she thought, that sounds properly interested without being *too* interested in the very fact he was returning. Odd, though, and disconcerting, that the very mention of his name sent that electric feeling racing through her veins.

The small fire snapping cheerfully in the fireplace, the warmth of the brandy, the comfort of being safe at last, began to spread a slow lethargy over Jennifer as the questions went on. Only her heart kept that excited beating under her ribs.

Abruptly, Angelina leaned forward, eyes perceptive. "We shouldn't be doing this to you. You're exhausted. How unfair we are! But it's only because we're so concerned about what happened. But it can wait, we'll hear the rest of it tomorrow when Scott arrives. You must get some rest now."

"I . . . I suppose I am tired," Jennifer said. "I've been so keyed up that I haven't been able to feel exhaustion. It's been . . . trying. Now I guess I'm beginning to feel it."

The rest of them rose, and Mario reached down a hand to bring Jennifer to her feet. "You've shadows under your eyes, my dear," he said, "and you look completely bushed. We've been thoughtless." He turned, picked up the brandy bottle, and smiled at her. "Perhaps a nightcap is indicated. To pull over your ears," he teased. "It will make you sleep better."

172

Jennifer shook her head. "Thanks, but no. The way I feel at this moment, I may just make it up the stairs and into bed before I fall asleep. If I took a brandy nightcap, I'd drowse off standing here."

Angelina joined Jennifer as she headed up the stairs. Mario, Jennifer noted, was staying behind with Constance. That, she thought, was good. Constance seemed relatively unscathed by Craig's guilt. Other than her quieter-than-usual demeanor, she seemed to have accepted the situation with a certain degree of calm. Jennifer wondered if Constance and Craig had been nearly as close as he had intimated. She thought not. Now there was no hindrance to a romance between Mario and Constance. The English girl had the money the Forlenzas so sorely needed, but, more than that, Jennifer suspected, if a marriage should take place, it would not be a loveless one, one of convenience.

Her thoughts were interrupted by Angelina saying, "You have no luggage, which I gather was left behind you, so you will need some basic toilet articles, nightgown, and perhaps a robe until you can get your own things back."

"Thank you," Jennifer said gratefully. "I'm really without anything."

Anything but a bedraggled appearance, Jennifer realized after entering her room and catching a glimpse of herself in the mirror. She looked absolutely awful! Hair matted and tangled, not visibly improved by her futile hand-brushing at the police station. Her clothes, shoes, dusty and disreputable, face drawn and pallid. Jennifer shook her head. No wonder the truck driver and policemen had given her those first doubtful stares.

A light tap at the door spun Jennifer around, and she hurried over to let Angelina in, the girl's arms laden.

"Are you certain there's nothing else you need?" she asked Jennifer as she draped the filmy white gown and negligee on the bed and set the toilet articles on the dresser.

"I'm certain," Jennifer said, lifting the gown and admiring it. "This is lovely!"

Angelina shrugged. "From my work. My designer is extremely generous with her models when the reviews and publicity are good. She gifts us with outfits, hoping we'll wear them in public, of course, so they'll be commented on." She wrinkled her nose delightfully. "Not lingerie, of course, other clothes."

"Angelina," Jennifer said, "was Constance upset by what happened to Craig? It must have been a shock, but she seems to be weathering it fairly well. I didn't like talking about him in front of her this evening as I did, but it all had to come out sooner or later. I didn't want to hurt her, but to answer questions, I had to say what he'd done."

"I wouldn't worry, Jennifer. Certainly she regrets what happened, we all do, and we dislike learning that someone we found amusing and entertaining was capable of such a terrible thing, but Constance had cooled on Craig before all this happened. She confided in me the day she moved in here that she was trying to break off with him gracefully."

"Then she wasn't in love with him?"

"Never. He knew she was coming to Italy, and she found him quite persistent in his attentions. She thought . . ." There was a faint show of color on Angelina's cheeks now. "She thought he was a fortune hunter and his affection was for her money more than for her."

Jennifer knew the reason for the reddening cheeks, but she brushed past any comment. "I'm glad, then, that she wasn't in love with him."

"No, I'm sure she wasn't," Angelina said, starting for the door. Just as she turned the knob, she said over her shoulder, "I do want to mention this. I answered the phone when Scott called the first time. About your vanishing. He was upset, very upset, and extremely worried, Jennifer."

"*And* angry. I imagine he was furious."

Angelina gave her a half-smile. "That he was! But he really was worried. His fear was that something might happen to you while you were alone. He didn't know then about Craig, of course. Anyhow, I did want you to know how concerned he was." With that she left, closing the door softly behind her.

Now, why had Angelina made such a point of telling her that about Scott? Jennifer stood still, the nightgown in her hands, face thoughtful. The only explanation she could think of was one that made her acutely uncomfortable. Had she been so transparent? How hard she'd tried to hide her emotions about Scott so no one would suspect. Had she failed? Was it so visible to the others? To Angelina?

And what about Angelina and Scott. Weren't they . . . hadn't they . . . ? *It was hers to announce,* Scott had said. Jennifer closed her eyes wearily; her brain simply wouldn't work anymore. She was too tired to think. Tomorrow, tomorrow, I'll figure it all out, she promised herself numbly.

In moments she was climbing into bed, snuggling comfortably into the pillow after turning off the light. She could make out the silvery moonlight edging around the heavy curtains, and she could hear the faint sounds from the canal. Then she slept.

But in the morning when she awakened, all the troubling thoughts and memories of yesterday were waiting for her, perched like birds of prey on the edge of her consciousness. Aching in bone and muscle from her escape over the uneven obstacle-studded fields, she struggled to a sitting position and looked about her.

The light edging the draperies at the French windows was not silver now, but gold, and she knew she'd slept a long time. Glancing at her watch, she found it had stopped. She shoved back the covers and walked unsteadily toward the bathroom to shower. Her head felt fuzzy from the still-present dregs of fatigue. Not yet, she told herself, don't try to reason it all out now, wait until you've showered, you'll feel better able to think clearly, you need to wake up.

But after the bath, there were no answers waiting for her. There was still no evident reason for Angelina's last comment. And, there was Scott. That was going to take some doing. Brisk, she thought—that's what she should assume, a brisk air. Not to become involved with him in arguments or to spend moments alone. Either one might be the catalyst that would lead her into betraying her feelings.

At least she wasn't going to have to face him as disheveled as she was last night. Wrapped in the large bath towel, she peered appraisingly in the mirror. Her hair once more burned with that reddish sheen, though still faintly damp. The shadows had gone from under her eyes, and the pallor had vanished.

There was a knock at the door, and Jennifer froze. Not Scott, not yet! She wasn't ready . . . not yet, and she certainly couldn't face him like this. Jennifer gazed down at the bath towel.

Haltingly she called, "Who is it?"

"Angelina!"

Going over to the door, Jennifer opened it a crack and peered out. Angelina stood there, a dress over her arm.

"Just until your own things arrive," the girl explained cheerfully. "I know you ruined the clothes you had on."

Jennifer swung open the door with one hand, the other clutching the towel about her. "Come in. I'm not very presentable, though."

Angelina smiled. "You'll find underthings and hose, too. They should fit; I think we're nearly the same size."

Jennifer felt a new rush of gratitude. How thoughtful and kind the Forlenzas all were. And Angelina . . . if Scott had to pick someone else . . . then Angelina . . .

To Jennifer's absolute horror, she heard herself saying, "Angelina, you and Scott . . . are you . . . I mean . . . in love? Engaged?" Then her face flamed. "Oh, I'm sorry, please forgive me, I didn't mean to ask, I shouldn't have said that!"

To her surprise and relief, Jennifer saw that Angelina seemed not at all perturbed; in fact, she was smiling.

"That's perfectly all right, Jennifer. But . . . whatever gave you that idea?" Angelina asked curiously.

"Scott said, that is, I thought he said something about your being the one to announce . . . that you were the one who should say . . ." Jennifer's voice stumbled painfully and trailed off into embarrassed silence.

For a moment Angelina didn't speak, her face thoughtful. Then she said slowly, "I think I understand. He didn't say exactly what I was to announce?"

Jennifer shook her head, still distressed. She hadn't meant to sound prying.

"Scott knows, though I hadn't intended him to, nor anyone else, really, not yet. It all came about because I inadvertently made a foolish *gaffe*—'spilled the beans,' as you Americans so graphically express it." Angelina's words were light, but her expressive eyes were serious. "Quite clearly, Scott didn't reveal it. I hadn't expected that he would. And I would ask you not to, until . . . such a time as my plans can be accomplished."

"Please don't . . . I mean, don't tell me, whatever it is, if you'd rather not," Jennifer said remorsefully, clutching at the towel that showed an inclination to slip.

Angelina smiled, a gentle smile. "No, I think, for many reasons, it's better that you know. It's not a great revelation, but I prefer not saying anything publicly yet. My present contract with the designer I work for is due to end in four more months. When that time comes, I plan not to accept another contract."

Jennifer listened, a puzzled expression on her face. She did not interrupt or even say a word when the other girl paused.

After a second's hesitation, Angelina continued, "I have decided to leave the secular world, at least for a time, and enter the religious life. I should like to teach or do nursing, preferably in the missionary field. I prefer it not be open knowledge now, lest it create publicity, you know"—her slender shoulders lifted in the trace of a shrug—"gossip-column fodder. 'Fashion Model Becomes Nun!' That distasteful sort of thing."

"But . . . Angelina, you're so beautiful . . . so . . ." Jennifer burst out.

"I'd be a hypocrite if I didn't admit that it is my appearance that is responsible for my fashion job," Angelina said quietly. "But I can't claim my features are my own doing, it's pure heredity. But inner beauty and serenity—that's what is far more important. And, a little harder to obtain," she added, her voice light once again. "Besides, it may not work out for me, yet I must try, Jennifer. I have the feeling of what some people term 'a call,' and I must answer, to find out for myself if this is what is meant for me."

Jennifer was having a hard time rearranging her thinking, this was all so surprising, so unexpected. And, all along, she had thought . . .

"What was Scott's reaction?" Jennifer asked curiously.

"He answered about in the same manner as the expression on your face. Astonished, half-disbelieving, and he asked me if I were sure. I told him no, not sure, but I had to find out for myself, in my own way. I'm not the first female in the Forlenza family to take this step. A great-aunt of mine was the most recent. But, anyhow, that's the big secret."

Turning toward the door, Angelina said, "By the way, Scott hasn't arrived yet." She eyed Jennifer's face; then her eyes began to twinkle at Jennifer's sudden confusion.

After she had gone, Jennifer walked dazedly over to pick up the clothes and dress for breakfast. So much had changed in the past forty-eight hours, there was no way she could put it together in her mind. It was like some absurd mixed-up form of musical chairs. Craig was being held by the police, Constance and Mario seemed almost fated to fall in love, Angelina. . . . *Angelina*—that was startling. How busily Jennifer's mind was skirting from one name to the other, so carefully avoiding the one that was most disturbing.

But she couldn't evade thinking about him for any length of time, so while she was zipping the light-wool pale-yellow frock, she reluctantly let Scott enter her mind and take over. What was she going to do about him? She was going to greet him coolly, distantly. Perhaps she might grudgingly apologize for escaping him on the train. Or should she? Jennifer gazed at herself in the mirror. Why was it, she wondered, when she tried to think logically about him, she invariably ended by seeing the gray eyes, the firm curve of his lips?

An uncomfortable thought struck her. Why had Angelina given her that amused look, what had caused that knowing twinkle in her eyes when she had mentioned Scott? Come to think of it, hadn't Mario done almost the same thing last night?

Jennifer turned from the mirror. Surely she hadn't been so transparent. Or . . . had she? The thought wasn't the most comforting one to carry with her as she descended the stairs to breakfast. Hopefully, Scott wouldn't be there; she needed a little more breathing time.

He wasn't. Constance and Angelina were having breakfast. Mario, they said, had gone to the police station.

"A Sergeant Mancini left word that you might be needed a little later," Angelina said, reaching over to fill Jennifer's coffeecup. "Mario said to tell you a report had come in that they captured the two men who had kept you prisoner. He didn't have any details."

"You look much more rested this morning," Constance said. She leaned across the table. "Did you hurt yourself? I didn't notice last night, but I see a faint bruise on your cheek when you turn your head a certain way."

Jennifer lifted her hand to touch the place Craig had hit her. She had not noticed it this morning either, but there was a slight tenderness under the skin when she put her fingers on it. "It's nothing," she said. "It doesn't really hurt. I . . . I . . . just bruised it a little." Jennifer couldn't bring herself to say what had really happened.

The three of them talked for a while; each of them appeared trying to lighten the atmosphere by discussing other subjects than the kidnapping. After a little, Constance left to go to her room.

"Jennifer."

Jennifer put her coffeecup down on the saucer as she lifted her head, to see Angelina's lips vainly attempting to control a ripple of laughter that suddenly escaped. "Oh, Jennifer," the Italian girl said, "please don't! Ever since you've come downstairs, you've been treating me so delicately, so . . . so . . . respectfully! I don't have a halo

yet, there hasn't been any public groundswell to elevate
me to sainthood. I'm Angelina Forlenza! Remember?"

"Have I really?" Jennifer looked startled. "I suppose I
have, unconsciously. It's just that I'm having trouble getting my mind into gear today. Would it help if I make an
effort to be abysmally rude to you for the next half-
hour?"

"Be my guest!" Angelina bowed her head politely from
across the table.

They both started laughing, and for the rest of the
time their conversation was lighthearted and, Jennifer
realized gratefully, didn't involve the name of Scott.

Angelina had household affairs to tend to after breakfast, and Jennifer drifted up to her own room. Strange,
she thought, how acute her hearing had become; the
sudden sound of a door opening and closing, the echo of
footsteps, brought her up tight, listening.

Crossing her room, she started wondering about having
to go to the police station. Or would a policeman come
here to question her further? Walking out onto the balcony, Jennifer looked over the city, thinking about the
kidnapping, yet trying to put it out of her mind, too.

Then, turning to go back into her room, she halted,
heart jolting. There he was, standing in the doorway of
the room he had occupied before, looking at her, eyes
enigmatic, hands stuck on his hips.

A thousand emotions flooded inside her, but she drew
herself erect and blurted sharply, absurdly, "You're a fine
bodyguard!" A wavering breath, then: "And a rotten detective!" She didn't mean it, not a word of it, but she had
to say something, anything! She was too throbbingly
aware of him to be sure of herself.

The gray eyes were blazing. Coming forward to stand
in front of her, Scott flared back, "And you, my dear
girl, acted like a stupid donkey! Very big joke you pulled,
wasn't it? The police told me your whole story. You
could have been murdered, you know, and I'll be damned
if you didn't practically invite it by trying to slip out of
the train, right into the trap that was laid for you. Not
very clever!"

The tension between them quivered. For a full minute they stood, barely a foot apart, looking at each other, hands gripping tight at their sides, nostrils flaring slightly from uneven breathing. Then, to Jennifer's dismay, she felt her eyelids sting and an infuriating tear or two well over and slide down her hot cheeks. She wanted to reach up and wipe them away, but stubbornly resisted, not wanting him to see her give in to emotion.

Then, suddenly, she was in his arms, caught close, his head bent to press against her hair. "You damned little dummy, I was out of my mind with worry!" His voice was husky. "Don't ever try anything like that again!"

"I . . . I . . . you're a fine one to talk, you . . ." she began indignantly, her voice trembling, not certain at all what she was saying, afraid to think, afraid to hope, afraid not to.

"Shut up!" he said rudely. "Keep your mouth closed for a minute. Every time you open it, we have a fight. Besides . . ." Reaching, he tilted her chin, his lips coming down on hers gently, then possessively.

As he lifted his head, Jennifer stared at him, dazed. "But . . . but . . . I thought . . ."

"That's the trouble," Scott said. "It has been, ever since the first. You start thinking, mostly about how to get the better of me, one way or the other." His voice was stern, but his cheek was laid against hers, his arms still held her close. "I'm never going to let you out of my sight again.

"From the first minute when I got on the plane and saw those big blue eyes, right then, despite the warning from your uncle to keep it all business, I was thinking: My God, this is it! This is the girl! And what happened? You came right out with the big freeze. You made it plain, buzz off! Hands off! What'd you expect in return?"

"What I got, I guess," Jennifer said in a very small voice. But she couldn't resist adding with a flick, "I got the big macho act!"

"See, what'd I tell you?" He lifted his head to look

down in her eyes. "The minute you start to talk, you start to argue, get feisty!"

"I . . . I . . ." she began indignantly.

"You want me to stop you from talking again?" he asked gruffly.

"Please," Jennifer said meekly.

He complied, his lips coming down again to capture hers, until they were interrupted by applause. Looking up, Jennifer saw a fat Italian man on a balcony on the opposite side of the canal, waving at them and cheering them on.

She hurriedly pulled away from Scott, but he tried to hold her. "Don't be foolish, Jennifer, all Venetians love love! He's demonstrating happiness for us, not jeering!"

She smiled weakly. "All the same, I'm not used to having people shout 'Brava!' when I'm being kissed."

Scott's eyes flickered a glance of dry amusement at her. "Very well, let's go inside."

They did, entering Jennifer's room, but she fended him off breathlessly. "Just a minute, Scott, I'm so . . . so mixed up. Everything's so . . . so . . ."

"So simple," he said. "People fall in love every day."

"In love," she repeated, then said it again. "In love? Are you, I mean, do you really . . . ?" She was getting more and more mixed up, her emotions clouding her thinking. But she finally managed, "People don't fall in love this quickly!" Then she felt hypocritical. *She* had. Days ago.

"Oh?" he replied. "Do tell! How about five minutes? That's what it took me. But, frustrating, my God, what did it get me? Not only the cold shoulder, the touch-me-not, but a Latin lover in the offing. From all I could see, you weren't exactly fending him off. So all I could do was try to keep you from finding out. I felt like a damned lovesick idiot."

"But you never said. How could I know?" Everything inside her was shining suddenly.

"Look back and tell me. There wasn't a time I could let you know, was there? You were either irritated at me or mooning with Mario. I didn't dare expose how I felt!"

"Scott," Jennifer confessed, "it was the same for me,

almost from the first. I tried to cover it up, too, for I thought you and Angelina . . ."

"What a rotten, rotten waste of time for both of us," he muttered. "Let's make up for it." Pulling her to him once again, he kissed her warmly, arousing a response in her that left her shaken.

"Please, just a minute, let me get my breath," Jennifer gasped unevenly when she pulled away. "Sit over there in the chair." She pointed. "Just for a little bit." She was trying to still the wild pounding of her heart. "When . . . when did you know I'd been kidnapped?"

He took the chair reluctantly, sighing. "All right, if you insist, but I'd really like to get back to making up for lost time. You've been the unapproachable snowmaiden up until now."

As Jennifer sat on the small sofa some distance from him, she saw him grimace; then he sighed again before speaking. "You're a difficult woman, Jennifer, but here goes: When I found you weren't in the compartment, I talked to the conductor, who said you had left the train. By yourself. Then I tried talking to other conductors, porters, on the trains and in stations. I hit it lucky when the conductor on the Florence run recalled a 'pretty American young lady' who seemed to be traveling with two gentlemen who were occupying the same compartment, but who had gone when he went through after the Bologna stop. The thing that really shook me was when he said you were alone at first, then joined by the two men. But, good Lord, where was I to go from there? The Bologna police were helpful, they sent men out searching, but they didn't have much to go on."

But . . . Craig, Jennifer thought. It seemed incredible, even now. Who would ever have suspected Craig? Then she realized it was Scott who had first suspected him. But he had also suspected Mario—even more, really. She started to say something, then didn't.

Scott leaned forward, hands braced on his knees. "I suppose there will have to be questions, details for you to take care of in connection with the police, Jennifer, but then . . ." Scott halted, looking at her.

"Then what?" she asked.

"We can't go on staying here forever. I've got a funny feeling that with you out of the picture, Mario may have a bit of courting to do. He was leaning that way. That is, you are out of the picture, I hope."

"Oh, I was never in it, really. He understood, right from the first, before I came over, that . . ." Then she flushed, meeting the look in Scott's eyes. "Well, he changed. It startled me. I didn't expect him to be so . . . so demonstrative."

"For a while it didn't look like you objected, but that's past. We still have about three weeks to go, remember. I promised your uncle I'd do bodyguard duty for four complete weeks, and you know how your uncle is about getting the job done. So you pick out where you want to go, and I'll trail along. Besides"—Scott turned suddenly serious—"there's always the possibility there was some truth to the kidnap rumor. Something could still happen. There was that fellow at Florian's, for instance."

Jennifer was on the verge of repeating her long-familiar plaint about her father's ever-present tendency toward unjustified alarm. It was exactly her father's reaction to the silly rumor that had triggered Craig into doing what he did. But she refrained from saying anything. The man in Florian's was simply a traveler, nothing more. She was convinced of that. Someday Scott might understand her uncle and her father.

She became aware that Scott's eyes were on her, and she looked up at him, to see an expression that started her now-slowing heart racing again.

"You know, Jennifer, I must consider more careful supervision of you in the future. You really aren't dependable, with that tendency of yours to sneak out late at night, as well as more serious AWOL activities. I don't trust you. Maybe we'd better rethink a bit. Is that offer of a cot in your room still open?"

Jennifer started to say something, hesitated, then blurted out, "That was supposed to be a joke! If you're suggesting meaningful relationships, if that's what you have in mind, you'd better think again."

He got up to stand in front of her, reaching down to bring her to her feet, just inches from him, his eyes flickering with amusement. "I'm surprised at you, Jennifer, to infer such a thing. To quote someone we both know, 'My intentions are strictly honorable.' " He pulled her to him and bent to kiss her, but was halted by a knock at the door and a voice calling.

It was Angelina. "Jennifer, the police phoned, they would like you to come to the station. They're sending a police launch for you."

"I'll be right down," Jennifer called back, her voice lilting now.

"Not without me," Scott whispered. Then he grinned down at her. "You know, Jennifer, my love, I've just had a reassuring thought. I guess I can stop worrying about losing my job. Uncle Henry can't possibly consider firing a relative!"

Jennifer gave him a sharp jab of the elbow as she brushed past him, heading for the door.

He took her arm, pinning it close to his side as they went out into the hall. From the open window in back of them came the shrill whistle of a *vaporetto,* and in the distance a church bell was chiming the hours.

ABOUT THE AUTHOR

Mary Ann Taylor began writing in the 6th grade and eventually became editor of her high-school paper. Professionally, her career began with a book-review column in an advertising newspaper and with the reviewing of books for women's groups. She soon became editor of a small-town weekly for which she wrote everything except the advertisements. Next came articles and then short stories, of which she has sold more than two hundred. Her poetry has been awarded prizes, and she has had five novels published to date.

Mary Ann Taylor lives with her retired Army Colonel husband in Carmel Valley, California. Throughout their married life they have also resided in such diverse places as Verona, Italy, and Alaska. Between the two of them, they have four children and nine grandchildren. Mary Ann loves to travel and her favorite hobby is cooking.